African Folk Tales

Folk Tales of Bogo People
From
Togo, West Africa

by

Kwaku A. Adoboli

RoseDog Books
PITTSBURGH, PENNSYLVANIA 15238

RoseDog Books
585 Alpha Drive
Suite 103
Pittsburgh, PA 15238
Visit our website at *www.rosedogbookstore.com*

ISBN: 978-1-4809-8013-6
eISBN: 978-1-4809-8036-5

FOLK TALES

What they are.

Folk tales are Oral Literature. They are not Short Stories or Novels. Folk Tales are not measured (judged) by the standards of Short Stories and Novels. They are short, action stories. There are no descriptive situations or character developments. Most are Fables—where animals behave like human beings, hence the pronouns are human ones.

Objectives:

Folk Tales are means of entertainment

Folk Tales are means to expound Wisdom

Folk Tales are meant to instruct the young

Folk Tales are also means to socialize the young into the norms and Culture of their Society.

Plots:

Folk Tales do not have Plots. They are the Plots. Around these Plots one can build a Short Story or a Novel. A vividly told Plot is a folk tale. Folk Tales are Myths and Fictions. How they are told!

They are action stories, told in direct short sentences. The audience, in front of the story teller, is more important than the stories. The teller reflects the actions and the moods of the story. The teller sings or dances along with the story, or gets the audience to join in. Folk tales are not told the same way twice. Each time something is added or detracted here or there to embellish the story. The same story may be told in four minutes or in twenty minutes.

The audience:

The audience is very important. Members are the ones being entertained or educated. The group is invited to sing, dance, ask questions or applaud a canning situation. The audience is an active one.

Types of Folk Tales:

Folk Tales may be Praises, Insults, Satires, Sarcastic observations, Hopes, Disappointments, Love, Joy, Celebrations, Hilarious or Canning. They may also be Proverbs (adages), Metaphor (figure of Speech), Literal, Indirections, Irony, Allusions, Innuendos, Circumlocutions (Evasive talks), or Nonsensical Rhymes. Some are about Heroes and Legends, Allegorical or symbolic characters and Puzzles.

Research:

1 The author went to well known tales tellers' homes, listened to them tell the folk tales, then wrote them down.

2 Where it was possible, the tales were recorded verbatim, on tapes, as they were being told. The tapes were later transcribed by the author.

3 In both methods the tales were written down in

IGO language of the Bogo People, then translated into English by the author.

4   All American based tales were composed by the author.

CONTENTS

Why No One Has
a Monopoly Over Knowledge

Listen to a tale!

We are ready for a tale!

In the far away land of Gossips, Rumors, and Innuendoes there lived a wise man. He was the philosopher who knew the answers to every problem. At the town squares and gatherings, the people turned to him to solve their problems, and to advise them on their needs and wishes. Among the town folks a few began imitating him as well as advising the people. After a while not many people came to seek his advice. He was no longer getting the adoration and glory as before.

One day he decided to hide the knowledge from others. No one else would know, advise or solve problems. The praises would be all his. He decided where to hide the

1

knowledge. He picked a tall palmetto tree in the town square and decided to put the knowledge way up among the leaves. He put all the knowledge and wisdom in the world in a big glass bottle, hanged the bottle around his neck, put it in front of him, and started to climb the tree. But every time he tried, the big glass bottle came between him and the tree. He tried several times and several times he failed.

Since the palmetto tree was in the town square, many people standing by were watching him. Of course, they did not know what was in the bottle. After another frustrating failure, a little girl, about six years old, stepped forward and said, "Hey Mister! Hang the bottle on your back, and you will easily climb the tree."

He followed the advice and began to climb the tree but half way up he became ashamed of himself. Here was a little child that had knowledge he did not have. He came down from the tree. In profound shame and anger, he smashed the big glass bottle on the ground. The bottle broke scattering knowledge all around. That is why we now have knowledge all over the world.

The Hunting of the Members

Those attentive, hear a tale!

May we hear a tale!

In the days of yore, the members (parts) of the body became dismembered, and went their separate ways. Only the chest and the belly were left together, eating was the only thing they did. The eye, the ear, the hand, and the leg were separate entities, and went around individually. One day they set out to hunt.

On the way, they engaged in a lively conversation on how hard the hunting would be. The eye said the moment he saw an animal and blinked, his eye brows would become arrows, pierce the animal, kill it, and it would be his. The ear boasted that he could spread and become as large as that of an elephant. Fanning the elephantine ear would

3

create a tornado that would knock down the animal, kill it, and it would be his. The hand said all he had to do was to touch the animal with a finger, kill it, and it would be his. The leg responded that when he walked to the animal, kicked it, it would be dead, and it would be his.

They were still on the way to the hunting ground while holding the conversation. Suddenly, the ear heard something, the eye saw it, the leg chased it till it reached the animal, the hand wrestled it down, and killed it. But they all forgot that they were separate parts of the body, traveling individually. The hunting was coordinated but when they realized they were separated, they began to fight over the hunt.

The ear said he heard it first, therefore it was his. The eye said he saw it therefore it was his. The leg cried foul and said, "you ear, you heard it but did not move; eye, you saw it but stayed put. I the leg ran after it, therefore it was mine." The hand exclaimed he could not believe what he was feeling. When the leg got to the animal, the leg did nothing. It was he the hand that wrestled down the animal and killed it, therefore it belonged to him. The members quarreled and almost got into a fight.

However, they decided to take the case to town for a judgment by the town folks. They picked the hunt and set out on the return journey. On the way back the ear began singing:

Hunting we went

If ear did not hear would eye see it

If eye did not see would the leg run after it

If leg did not run would the hand catch it

If hand did not catch it would we have a hunt

Hunting we went.

Eventually the members arrived at the King's Court. The ear sang the song before the King. The members put out their case to be judged. The King and his elders analyzed the case. Then the Mouth who was the spokes person for the King, stood up, and rendered the judgment. The judgment was for the ear. The other members became angry and left.

From that day, the mosquito would come every night to tell the ear, "you won the case." Whenever the mosquito came to say this, the hand would swap it away, saying, "get out of here, you biased fellow."

These were the words of a song my grandmother sang for me when I was a little kid, now I pass them onto you!

Why the Smoky Mountains Smoke

Believe it or not, this story happened!

Let's hear the knots and bolts of the story!

Long, long ago, in the days of our great grandfathers and great grandmothers, Native Americans, Europeans, and Africans settled in the Low Country of South Carolina. They were hard working people who fished, farmed and traded along the coast. They caught crabs, shrimps and bass from the coastal waters. On the farms they grew rice, sugar cane, indigo, tobacco and later cotton. These farm products were sold to people in the far away lands, across the oceans. Life was good to some and very harsh to others. The coastal plain was as flat as a table top, no mounds, hills or mountains. The people had never seen or heard about mountains.

The Native Americans brought fur to the coast to trade for guns, knives, and other things. Some of the settlers went with the Natives to the hinterlands, far from the coast. These settlers became trappers roaming the woods as far as the present day Greenville and Ashville. They were amazed by the mountains and the perpetual, continuous smoke coming out of them. They came back with stories of lands that rose up high, all the way to the sky. The farmers, fishermen and traders did not believe these stories. How could lands rise high up to the sky, they asked. They declared the trappers had too much to drink and smoke.

As time went on, more and more stories of the gigantic mountains and their habit of smoking came back to the Low Country. The Native Americans also repeated these stories. The people became interested, their curiosity rose, they wanted to see these things for themselves.

The news spread like wild fire that they would like to go to see the lands in the sky. The date for the expedition was set. Early that morning about fifty people gathered on Bay Street, Beaufort, SC. for the memorable journey. In those days, trains, buses, or cars did not exist, people walked everywhere. As they walked they came to the Whale Branch river and crossed it at a low tide. At Yamassee more people joined them, and the group headed for Charleston, SC. through Walterboro.

In Charleston, they were joined by hundreds of people from the city, Edisto, Folly Beach and Mount Pleasant. Every night they would camp, make wood fires, cook and eat. Entertainment consisted of drumming, singing, dancing and story telling. All kinds of people were on the expedition: boys and girls, mothers and fathers, grand parents, neighbors, strangers, farmers, fishermen, lawyers, and trappers who led the way.

By the time the group got to the present day Columbia, their numbers had swelled up to include ministers, school teachers, and a few politicians. The journey continued along foot paths, byways and trade routes until they got to the lands of Spartans. The Spartans who lived in burgs (cities) knew the mountains, and offered to lead the expedition the next morning. Early morning, over nine hundred people gathered in front of homes and forts of the Spartans and set out to the Western Lands. The sky was clear and the weather pleasant on that September morning. Suddenly, there! Right in front of them were the lands that rose up all the way to the heavens. They could not believe their eyes. The spectacles, the majesty of the mountains, the smokes, were overwhelming.

The people began to walk faster and shouting in disbelieve. Soon the quick walk became running. They ran towards the mountains and at the feet began climbing them.

In their eagerness to get to the top, parents were separated from their children, loves ones forgot each other, it was every one for himself. As they climbed higher and higher up the mountains, the smokes became heavier and heavier, and the air hotter and hotter. The excitement, the novelty of it all out weighed any discomfort they felt, so on they went. They climbed up to the heavens, to the top of the mountains, right into the thick, heavy hot smokes.

The smokes were hot but the people saw no flames, and saw no burning bushes. They ran around the plateaus of Ashville, Cherokee, Gatlinburg and Pigeon Forge, but saw no ashes, no flames, and no fires. The mountains continued spewing out hot fumes and hot smokes. The people were perplexed. Finally, THERE SHE WAS! Right on the very top of Mount Pisgah, sat an old Native American Grandmother, smoking a forty five foot long PIPE. All the smokes, all the ashes, all the heat, and all the commotion, were from this one GREAT PIPE. They named the places SMOKY MOUNTAINS, and to this day it is said, "if you go there early in September, you will see this Grandmother smoking away her PIPE."

Meat Eating Plants
on Lady's Island

Here is a true story!

By all means, may a true story be told!

In the summer of 1999, a crook, a bad man, robbed a bank on Bay Street, Beaufort, South Carolina. Bay Street was the main street in down town Beaufort. Several shoppers as well as tourists were in the street when the robbery occurred that fateful day. The bad man came out of the bank with bags in hand. The police siren could be heard coming from the direction of the Federal Court House, a bank clerk had called the police. The bank clerks stepped outside, shouting and pointing at the bad man. The man tried to mingle among the crowd but finally ran across The Woods Memorial Bridge, on foot. The city police followed in hot pursuit, in two patrol cars. The crowd gathered at Henry C. Chamber Water Front Park, watching the spectacle.

There was great excitement and expectation of seeing the criminal brought back by the police. More police cars crossed the Bridge. Beaufort County Sheriff Deputies and the State Troopers could be seen crossing the Memorial Bridge as well as the Port Royal Bridge to Lady's Island. K-9 unit also zipped by. About thirty minutes later, police helicopter appeared zigzagging the Island sky. But there was no sign of the criminal.

Afraid the bad man might catch a ride or hijack a car, police closed the traffic to and from Lady's Island. After a while the traffic was opened and the police searched each car. However, the searches yielded nothing. People began to wander, how could a man on foot, in hot pursuit by the police, disappear without a trace.

The NBC affiliate, channel 3 in Savannah, Georgia, broadcast the news along with the robber's pictures taken by the bank cameras. The Beaufort Gazette and the Island Packet carried the news next morning. The public was warned, the bad man was dangerous and carried a gun. Lady's Island residents panicked, they would not let any unknown face into their yards.

On the fourth day, radio and TV stations flashed the news. Human bones were discovered under a big oak tree near Lady's Island Airport. The description of the bad man by the clerks, led the Sheriff to suspect the gun and clothing found near the bare bones belonged to the robber. The coroner sent the bones to the Medical University of South Carolina in Charleston for an autopsy. The results came back in two days confirming the suspicion. The results deepened the puzzle. How did a healthy, vibrant man with the energy to escape from the police become bare bones in four days?

In their puzzlement, confusions, and discussions some people remembered Rudy of South Carolina ETV. Rudy was a naturalist who came to the Sea Island from time to time. He identified just about anything, and talked about meat-eating plants, such as venues flytraps and pitcher plants. Rudy was called from Columbia, South Carolina. He came right away. With the deputies and curious on lookers he proceeded to the County airport and to the big oak tree where the bare bones were found.

In ten minutes Rudy solved the puzzle. Under the giant oak tree were several venues flytraps and pitcher plants. The robber, seeking to hide from the police, lay down among the plants, unaware of the dangers. The plants immediately engulfed him, preventing his being seen. In four days, the meat-eating plants devoured him, flesh by flesh, leaving the bare bones for the coroner to pick.

Doubt this story at your own risk!

How the Atlantic Ocean was Formed

Here is a tale begging to be told!
By all means, tell us the tale!

A great many years ago, large dragons roamed up and down the State of South Carolina. Everywhere they went a trail of water followed them. The foaming from the mouths of these large and scary dragons became water, and the trail of water became rivers. The rivers ran behind the dragons wherever they went.

One particularly large dragon, called Broad, ran from Gaffney toward Columbia. Another similarly large one, called Saluda, ran from Greenville to Columbia. The two met in the valley below the Governor's Manson near the Riverbank Zoo. Each claiming the right of way, they began to fight. In their mortal struggle, they did not see a third

17

huge foaming dragon bearing on them. This third dragon, called Congaree, swallowed Broad and Saluda. Congaree swelled up, became bigger, and continued roaming around. Everywhere Congaree went the foaming became water, and the trail of water became a running river. All dragons it met were swallowed up, it got bigger and bigger.

In those days there was a huge monster hanging around Charleston. The people called it Cooper. Cooper was ferocious, mean, and hated other monsters. It roamed around as far as present day Marion. One day the monster Cooper and the dragon Congaree met near Moultrie. They made loud noises and fought fearlessly. Cooper won, and swallowed Congaree up. Cooper continued roaming around and became bigger and bigger. It foamed a lot. The foam became water, and the trail of water came a river. Cooper retuned to Charleston, hanged around the Battery, and terrorized the people.

There was another huge monster called Ashley. Ashley too hanged around Charleston and terrorized the people. The citizens of Charleston lived in constant fear of the two monsters. One day the inevitable happened. The two monsters met, fought, chased each other around the Battery, James Island and Mount Pleasant. They made horrible noises. The two looked like huge crocodiles. The citizens of Charleston had enough of the monsters and decided to get rid of them. The Mayor volunteered to fight them. Early one morning, the Mayor got on a horse, grabbed his sword, chased the two monsters, and slew them. The monsters made horrible noises, foamed a lot, and finally died.

The enormous amount of foam flowing from the two monsters became waters. The waters joined together at the Battery and became the Atlantic Ocean. Now that you know how the Atlantic Ocean was formed, go create your own tale.

What Dogs, Cats, and Politicians Have in Common

Here is a believable story!

May a believable story be told!

Once upon a time dogs and cats were wild animals that lived in the jungles. They had to hunt all day and every day for their food. The hunts were dangerous and tiresome. One day the dogs called a pow wow to discuss their plight. They came from distant forests, over the hills and mountains, large dogs, small dogs, black, white, spotted, and mixed colors. The objective was to find a solution to their situation.

Among the questions discussed were why should they, self respecting dogs, live in the jungles? Why should they be exposed to rain, cold, snow or alligators in warmer climates? Some even asked why suffer in the wild while human beings lived in homes, in comfort and in luxury? One fellow said, "let us go and enslave human beings and become their masters." This was considered a lofty objective but how were they going to achieve it. After an all day discussion, they decided to go to human beings and tell them, "we dogs are willing to be your servants and you be our masters, we will serve you faithfully and you will feed, cloth, and shelter us." All the dogs did exactly that, the human beings believed they had servants in their homes.

The dogs knew better. They knew the were the masters. They did practically nothing in the homes. They sat around being lazy all day long. Human beings housed, fed, and protected them. They even took the dogs to the doctors when sick.

Not long after, cats too called pow wow. They had seen the success of the dogs: stoop to conquer. Cats came out of the jungles and into the homes, huts, mansions, and palaces to lord it over human beings. The cats did practically nothing, just sat there being lazy all day long. Some even developed attitudes, when called, they would not come immediately. They would showed up at their own time.

The race of human beings called politicians saw the success of the dogs and the cats. They went to other human beings and said, "look we are the same as you, we belong to the same stock, we live, speak, laugh, and play just like you. Let us be your servants and you be our masters. We will serve you in every way: in City Halls, County Councils, Legislatures, and Congresses. Just elect us, and be willing to be our masters."

Other human beings, unaware of the plot, agreed. From that day even to this day, politicians went about calling themselves, "Public Servants." But since when has any politician come to serve you, be your servant, or even listen to you!

Look Out Mountains
of Chatanooga

Believe this tall story at your own risk!

We are willing to risk!

Once upon a time a race of people settled in that part of Tennessee called Chatanooga. They originally came from beyond the seas and now lived in the valleys and on top of the mountains. They loved to fish in the Tennessee River and also grew corn along the creeks. But one thing they loved most was swimming in the river. Those living on top of the mountains came down to the valleys, to down town Chatanooga, to swim in the river. They would swim all day long, and in the evening, climb the mountains back to their abodes. They had beautiful homes, tree lined streets, and stores selling swimming gear.

Even though the mountain top dwellers were arrogant and condescending, others in Chatannoga and in the valleys did not consider them very smart. Their preoccupation with swimming left no time for involvement with their neighbors.

The mountains and valleys were always full of fogs, particularly in the morning. The mountain top dwellers usually saw the fogs way down in the valleys in the morning. By the evening the fogs would dissipate. One day they woke up and saw the thick, heavy fogs had risen right up to the top of the mountains. They mistook the fogs for a flooded Tennessee River. Soon the word went round that the River had flooded and came up to them. It was time to go swimming.

A drummer boy went up and down the streets drumming:

Rap rapity rap rap rap

Rap rapity rap rap rap

Rapity rap rapity rap rap rap rap

Acting as the town crier, he rallied the people to go swimming. In no time the streets were full of people in swimming gear. In a celebrating mood, singing, dancing, and moving with rhythmic strides they soon arrived at the edge of this once in a life time flooded River. One by one they jumped into the River. As they jumped, the drummer boy continued drumming:

> *Rap rapity rap rap rap*
> *Rap rapity rap rap rap.*
> *Rapity rap rapity rap rap rap rap*

As the last citizen jumped, the drummer boy noticed the swimmers were not coming back. The fun was in the jumping, hence the people would have come back to jump several times. But not so today. None of them came back The drummer boy sensed something was wrong. He threw his drum into the River. He could hear the hollow drum rolling down the mountain:

> *Glong glong glo glo glo glong*
> *Glong glong glo glo glo glong.*

Suddenly, in horror, he realized what had happened. He ran down the mountain to Chatanooga to announce the tragic news. From that day on, visitors to the mountains were warned, "look out, don't go swimming," and the mountains were named, "Look Out Mountains."

Plain and Unnoticed Doers

Here is a tale begging to be told!
By all means, let it be told!

Not long ago, all animals called a Conference and a Social Gathering to be held on one of the Sea Islands off the coast of South Carolina. The Conference was held at the Famous Resort right by the Atlantic Ocean. They came from all over South Carolina: from the Old England, the Up States, The Low Country, and the Midlands. Each animal was adorned in splendor, in the finest costume of plume and fur. Among them were deer, bears, raccoons, rabbits, turkeys, ospreys and turtles.

The all day Conference was followed by the evening dinner, social and dance. The social gathering was around the pool, the lagoon, and the pavilion. Gentle evening breezes were provided by the Atlantic Ocean across from the pavilion. When it was time for the dance, a quartet of mocking birds from Charleston, South Carolina, provided the music. At the sound of the trumpets, all the animals stood up and began to dance. They danced from the pool to the lagoon, around the pavilion and back to the pool. Round and round they danced all evening. Grace and agility were displayed. They performed the latest dance crazes, the classics, as well as furious gyrations to forgotten rhythms.

The two legged employees watched this spectacle in awe and in amazement. The employees could not believe what they were seeing. They were out of words to express what was taking place.

As the animals whirled, jerked, and twirled round and round, they noticed that the Turtle was not dancing. He was just following them back and forth. Towards the end of the GUMBE Mr. Rabbit posed a question for all to hear, "Mr. Turtle, how come you are not dancing?" There upon, Mr. Turtle replied, "Mr. Rabbit, I am dancing, I am twirling, jerking, and grinding just like everybody else. It is the shell around me that prevents you from seeing my dance routine."

Sometimes, the mote may not really be in our eyes, but what we are looking at, may not be what we are seeing.

Why We Cannot Touch the Sky

Here is a tale!

May a tale be told!

Long, long ago, the sky was so close to earth you could touch it. The sky was beautiful, full of sunshine, and many splendid colors. There were also people of all races on every part of the earth. The people worked hard all day, and in the evening they sat down to sumptuous dinners. They ate with their fingers, the foods were finger-licking good. After the meals, they washed their hands, then wiped them dry against the sky. From years of abuse, the sky became wet, discolored, and dirty. The sky did not like this situation, hence it withdrew far away.

Now we cannot touch the sky. It looks so near yet so far to touch. We could go to the top of the highest mountains, see the sky very close, but unable to touch it. It is even said one can fly to the moon and still not able to touch the sky.

Forgiveness

Here is a horrible tale!

By all means, spin the yarn

This tale moved round and round and finally, landed on two young men. A great many years ago two young men went to a college, far away from home. One day the two friends went hiking in the forest. After a while they realized they were lost, tired, and hungry but continued the hiking. They came upon an old lady in her cottage in the woods. The generous lady received them with enthusiasm and cooked for them. While they were eating one of the young men picked the lone meat in the soup and ate it. The other young man became angry because he had no meat to eat. He hit the first young man with a big stick, broke his neck, and the young man died instantly. The second young man became afraid and began to run away.

The generous old lady seeing what happened, yelled and called her neighbors. When the good neighbors heard what happened, they ran after the second young man. The young man doubled up his speed and ran for his life. After a while, he came to a cottage at the bank of a big river. There was an old man sitting under a tree in the middle of his cottage, he was slowly weaving a basket. The young man asked for a safe haven from pursuers. When the old man inquired of his plight the young man replied that he would tell his story after the pursuers left. The old man agreed and hid the young man in one of his rooms in the cottage.

Soon after a host of the pursuing villagers arrived. They hardly completed exchanging greeting with the old man before they began asking him whether he saw a young man running towards the cottage. The old man replied that he saw no one. He then enquired from the villagers the cause of their anger, indignation and yelling.

The angry mob informed the old man that his only child, the first young man, he sent to college, was beaten to death by the other young man they were chasing. They were chasing the killer so they could avenge the death. After a long, anguish and sorrow, the old man told the pur-

suers that, in truth, he saw no young man. The old man asked them to go back and bury the dead. He added that if they found the killer they should forgive him, and not make any demand of him. The mob turned back in anger, indignation and yelling.

After all the pursuers left, the old man called the second young man out of the house and said, "be frank with me, why were the villagers chasing you." The second young man who had heard everything, explained the whole story to the old man. The old man said, "I forgive you, go your way, and don't commit sin anymore." If you were the old man, would you be able to forgive, and if you were the second young man, would you be able to tell the truth?

This was the yarn my grandfather told me and I too want to tell you. May those who hear it abide by it.

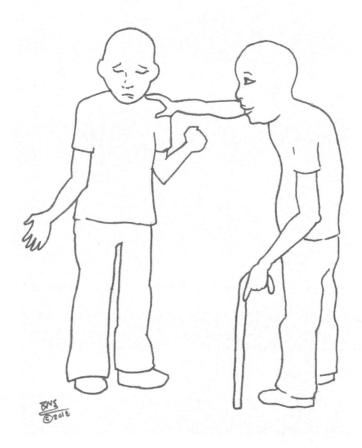

NOTE: The above questions were not whether the old man did the right thing or wrong thing; nor whether the young man was right or wrong in telling the truth. The question was what you, sitting here, would do in such situation.

Revenging a Dead Enemy
Is Not Strength

Here is a tale!

Let us hear a tale!

This tale staggered round and round and landed on a Lion, a Horse, and the rest of the Wild animals.

Not long ago, an old lion that was very wicked with other wild animals, laid prone by his den, dying of old age. When the other animals saw him, they had no pity on him. They ridiculed him and asked who would have a pity on this destroyer of peace.

The boar insulted the lion. The bull horned him, and asked, "weren't you devouring my children?" The pig with its canine teeth, left a gaping hole on the lion's side. Even the donkey kicked him several times. Several of the animals took their turns in revenge even after the lion died.

Only the horse stood by the lion, and did not harm it, even though this same lion had captured the horse's mother.

The horse, not revenging, amazed the donkey. So the donkey asked the horse, "don't you want to revenge?" After some agonizing moments the horse replied, "it is not right for me to vent my anger on an enemy who could no longer defend himself. Revenge on a helpless or dead enemy is not strength. But forgiveness is."

These are words of a LULABY my grandmother sang to me, and I pass them to you.

The Lion and the Mule

Here is a tale!

Let's hear a tale!

This tale involved the lion and the mule. Long, long ago, the lion and the mule lived in the jungle, and the lion was the king of all jungle animals. The lion used to prey on the mule's calves until there was only one left. The mule was very protective of the lone calf to a point where the lion could not catch it.

One day the lion went to the mule and asked to take the lone calf home to live with him. The mule agreed, for the lion was the king and had to be obeyed. The lion took the lone calf home. At night the lion put the calf to sleep next to the lion's kitten. Then when everybody was asleep, the calf took his clothes of wool and put it over the lion's kitten. He then put the kitten's clothes of wool over himself.

At dead of night, the lion came to get the calf. Naturally he picked the one with calf clothes on, and ate it. At day break the lion realized it was his own son he ate. However the lion was determined to eat the calf, and the calf too continued to play the trick on the lion. This went on night after night until the lion ate all his children.

On this last day, when all his children were gone, the lion gave the calf a gallon of corn to roast. He said the corn should be roasted so they would eat popcorn the next day. While the calf was roasting the corn, it sang the following song:

Pohna! Pohna!

I know what goes on at night!

That night, the calf secretly cut banana stump and laid it beside him. He put his clothes of wool over the stump and banana barks over himself. The lion came again. He immediately jumped over the supposed calf. The lion's claws got stuck inside the banana stump. While he was wagglying to get himself out, the calf ran away to its parents.

Friends, evil thoughts and evil acts will come back to hurt you. This is a nursery tale my grandmother once told me and I pass it over to you.

Why Plantain is Curved
and Banana is Short

Here is tale!

We are ready for a tale!

Once upon a time, Banana and Plantain were friends. Early one morning Plantain went to the home of Banana. After exchanging pleasant greetings, Plantain asked Banana why during storms he made so much noise that nobody could hear anything. Banana replied that he had no foggy idea what Plantain was talking about. Banana went on to ask whether Plantain just sat there, did nothing, during a storm. (Both of them had long broad leaves that blew in the wind).

Plantain demanded to know why Banana was disrespectful, did Banana not know that he Plantain was much older and wiser. Banana asked Plantain to get lost for he was in no mood for quarrelling, more over, he had not eaten breakfast that morning to listen to any raving from Plantain.

The heated quarrel became a fight to a point where both fell down. Before others arrived to separate them, Banana stood up, grasped Plantain, and punched him in the stomach. The punch was so hard that Plantain curved over his stomach. When Plantain steadied himself, he picked a big stick and hit Banana over the head. The blow was so hard that Banana became short. From that day Plantain became curved and Banana became short.

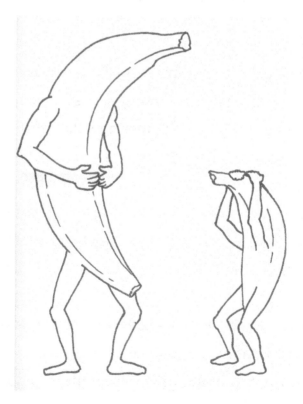

Why the Snake Has a Long Neck and the Crab Walks Sideways

Here is a tale!

May we hear a tale!

This tale fell on the snake, the crab, and the song bird. In ancient times the snake had a short neck and the crab walked straight forward like other animals. The crab came into a big debt and unable to pay back the loan. He had several sleepless night agonizing over the debt. Reluctantly he went to borrow money from the snake to pay the loan. After a long time when the crab did not pay back the loan, the snake went to ask for payment. The crab said he had no money to pay back the loan, and therefore the snake should wait a while longer. The snake went back home.

After a year, the snake had still not got his money, so he went to his friend, the song bird, pleading with the bird to collect the debt for him. The song bird said it had been a long dry season, hence the crab had not come out of his hole. As soon as it started to rain and crab came out, he would collect the debt for the snake. But the snake had no patience nor a desire to wait, he went to collect the debt. But the drought was still on, and the crab had not come out of his hole, so the snake went back home.

The rains finally came. The snake took the song bird along to collect the debt. On arrival the snake asked the song bird to go down the hole to demand payment of the loan. The bird refused. The snake was angered by this refusal and went down into the hole himself. The song bird knew what would happen, so he flew up and sat on a near by branch of a tree, listening to the two antagonists.

The moment the crab saw the snake he asked what was the snake's mission. The snake replied that he came to collect the overdue loan. The snake had not finished his statement when the crab grabbed him by the throat. The grab was so hard and so merciless that the snake started wiggling and both landed out side. The song bird begged the crab to let go the snake, after a while he did. But the snake neck became elongated. The song bird, watching the whole situation began to sing:

Aggressive debt collection will lead to pain

Aggressive debt collection will lead to pain.

To this day the crab never paid the debt. Every time the crab came out of his hole, people would be sneering at him, and urging him to pay the debt. Unable to face the people, the crab would run sideways to hide. This was how it came about that the snake had a long neck and the crab walked sideways.

Those who have ears to hear, hear!

Yes, we have learned a lesson!

Thou shall not be a borrower!

Thou shall not harass your debtors

They made you a creditor!

The Aged and Wisdom

In the mood for a tale?

We are ready for a tale!

This tale fell on the citizens of an ancient town. One day the young men in the town came together and decided that the old men and women (senior citizens) troubled them too much. The seniors always asked them to listen, obey and do things. The young men wanted to leave town with all their belongings, and establish a new town. Away from the travails of the seniors, everything would be alright.

Now, the elderly philosopher wanted you to open your ears and listen. The young men eagerly began to build the new town. Their thoughts and actions were coordinated so well that within six months, the new town was ready, and they moved in. The date for celebration of establishing the new town was set. The decoration and the beauty of the town were very impressive. The elderly in the old town were astounded and speechless. The youth were joyous and proud of their new town and accomplishment.

The youth were proud of the young man who suggested the new town that they made him a king to reign over them. More over, his father was a man of wisdom, and all the young man's advice came through. The same date was set for celebrating the new town as well as for installing the new king. The day came, talking drums summoned the youths, and the people gathered. The celebrations were high spirited and the new king was also installed. Visitors were amazed and overjoyed.

Now there was another wise youth among them, to whose advice they began to listen. He said before the king could achieve respectability and dignity among kings, he had to be clothed in sheep skin garments.

The garments, especially the wig, should be so white that the youthful king would look elderly. They agreed on this advice. They killed a large ram (male sheep), with white fleece. They removed the skin from the flesh and bones, and prepared it to look like a garment. This raw garment was put on the king. The youth did not know how leather was made.

The king in his new clothes looked spectacular. He was singularly white so they called him powdered old philosopher. The youths no longer went to the old town, and the elderly left behind too did not visit the new town. Young people, listen and hear. Exactly four days after the king's new garment, the robe became stiff and stuck on the skin of the king. No matter how hard they tried, they could not get the robe off him. The king was no longer free in his person. He was in serious pain. The youths did not know how to free him. To cut the garment with knife would entail cutting the king's skin. They thought of every means, but none would work. Yet if they king stayed in that robe for another day, he would die.

In anxiety and fear, they agreed to go back to the old town to ask for help from the elders. Yes, the olds had experience, they would go to them. The youths sent two delegates to the elders to explain what was going on. One elderly fellow came with the delegates, what he saw was not pleasant; the king was dying from suffocation. He advised them to get hammock and to carry the king to the river. On arrival, the king should be immersed in water, the sheep skin would soak (absorb) water, be soft, and ready to come off the king. He hardly finished talking when the youths took the king to the river and immersed him in water. The skin softened and was pulled off the king. The king came alive.

When they returned from the river, the king called a gathering and told them it would be better if they all return to the old town. He said they aught to go back, listen and obey the elders who had wisdom. If they did not, and something like that happened again, that would be the end of them. They left the new town and went back home to the elders.

This was a nursery story my grandfather once told me, may I pass it on to you.

The Consequences
of Uncontrolled Anger

Here is a sorrowful tale!

May we hear a sorrowful tale!

This tale was about uncontrolled anger and what followed from it. The tale involved around a man and his young daughter. The man was a vintner (wine maker) and his young daughter was about five years old. One day the young child got sick and was going to toilet several times. When she felt a little better she accompanied her father to the farm to check on the vines. At the farm she was left in the farm hut while the father was up and down among the vines. She got sick again and called the father. Whenever she was attacked by diarrhea and felt the urge to go to toilet she would call the father.

When she called the father one more time, he became

angry. He came to the child angrily and hit her in the stomach and said, "you are too much, I am tired of your going to toilet." When the daughter was hit in the stomach, she bent over and fell flat on the ground. It was a severe blow and painful, the child could not move. After a new moments the father called the little girl, but no response from the child. He quickly lifted the child up but she was bleeding from the nose. He called the daughter, but no response. The child was dead.

Dear friend, see where anger and impatience led this father. This was a tale my grandmother told me the other day when we were sitting on her front porch. I would like you too to hear it.

Whosoever Sets a Trap for his Neighbor Shall Eventually Fall into His Own Trap

Here is a tale!

We shall surely hear a tale!

This tale fell squarely on a squirrel and Yiyi or Ananse (the Spider).

A great many years ago, a severe drought fell on the land. It did not rain for over five years, the crops failed and famine reigned over the land. Several animals traveled long distances in search of food. Yiyi and his family too suffered from the famine. One day, while Yiyi was up and down the country side looking for food, he came across a very big stone. The stone had many eyes and was scary to look at. The moment he saw the stone he cried out loud, "Lord have mercy, I have met abomina-

53

tion, a misfortune! What a stone is this? And why many eyes." Yiyi almost fainted when he heard the stone speak. The stone ordered him to keep quiet and added that whoever called him, "stone-with-many-eyes" shall surely die. Immediately Yiyi was silent and kept his mouth shut. After a while Yiyi begged the "stone-with-many-eyes" to allow him to remove the stone from its location because the current place was not good for it. He said he would take the stone to a better location that was swept and cleaned.

The stone agreed and Yiyi took it to a junction on the main road. The stone was heavy but Yiyi carried it with difficulty to the new location, an intersection that all animals came across in their search for food. Yiyi went to hide behind a nearby tree. Whenever Yiyi saw an animal coming he would jump into the middle of the road and ask, "dear friend, look, what is that in the middle of the intersection? I am afraid of it."

Any animal that responded by saying that monster was a "stone-with-many-eyes" died immediately. Of course, the dead animal became food for Yiyi and his family. Yiyi went on with this trap throughout the years of the drought and famine. He and his family were well fed, strong, and prosperous. Until this day, the animals were not aware of this clever trap.

Only the squirrel knew about the trick Yiyi played on the other animals. The squirrel used to go from tree to tree through braches looking for food. He did not travel along the main road. The squirrel had observed Yiyi from the trees. He began to feel pity for the many animals that succumbed to the trap; and decided to do something about it. So one day the squirrel took the main road leading to the intersection.

Before he could get close to the "stone-with-many-eyes," Yiyi caught up with him, and asked the usual question. "Friend, look, what is that in the middle of the intersection?" Pretending he did not know anything, the squirrel replied, "dear friend, I have forgotten the name." Yiyi then replied, "friend, I will remind you, its name is "stone-with." The squirrel too replied, the name is "stone-with." Yiyi shouted at the squirrel saying, "finish the name." The squirrel too replied, "finish the name."

Yiyi waited for a while and said, "what!" The squirrel also waited for a while and thinking hard said, "stone-with," "stone-with." Yiyi shouted again at the squirrel, but alas, the squirrel stopped at "stone-with." The situation was not going as fast as Yiyi wanted. He got angry and shouted, "foolish squireel, you do forget things too much." Yiyi then stepped very close to the squirrel and whispered into his ears, saying it slowly and clearly, "stone-with-many-eyes." The moment the name fell from the mouth of Yiyi, he stumbled down and died. Yiyi fell into his own trap and died.

Whosoever sets a trap for his neighbors shall eventually fall into his own trap. The other day I went to help grand-mother at her home, she told me this story as a lesson. Now I pass it to you to think about it.

Knowledge is Like a Baobab Tree, Cannot Be Encircled with Hand

Listen to a tale!

May a tale be told!

This tale traveled far and wide, and finally landed on a King and a young man. A great King once lived in a far away Kingdom. He was renowned for wisdom, riches and justice. One day the King sent orders throughout his Kingdom saying that as a wise King, he would name all children born in the Kingdom. The King carried out his orders, named and misnamed several children.

The people had a tradition in naming children. A child was named after the day he or she was born. The child was not called by the name of the day he or she was born on, rather by one of the several names set aside for that day. Hence a boy born on Thursday

(Yaoda) was called Yao and one born on Sunday (Kwasida) was called Kwasi.

Eventually, one of the misnamed children grew up and refused to be known by the misnomer. He changed his name to "Wiserthan king." When the King heard the name, he was exceedingly displeased. The King decided to test the young man to see if he was indeed wiser than the King. If the young man was not wiser, he would be put to death. The young man was summed to the presence of the King for the test.

The King gave him one grape seed and ordered him to go plant it, harvest it, process it into wine, and bring him the wine, in gourd, the same day. Wiserthanking accepted the challenge and went home. On arrival home, Wiserthanking sent a messenger to the King, with one gourd's seed. The message was delivered to the King, saying that while Wiserthanking was on his way to plant the grape the King also should plant the gourd's seed. The King should plant it, tend to it, harvest it, and hallow it into a gourd and send it to "Wiserthanking" the same day. Wiserthanking would then put the wine into the gourd and bring it to the King.

The King was surprised by the wisdom displayed by the young man. He did not know what to say. However, the King conceived of another test that would sealed the fate of the young man. The King sent him to go and ask Mr. Death to build day and night. The young man should bring the day and night to the King. The young man did not understand the test but he set out on the journey.

The young man came to a large river where he saw a lot of birds swimming, drinking, singing, and just having a good time. He begged them for their feathers. Each bird gave him a little of its feathers, and they stuck the feathers all over him. Wiserthanking looked like a big, odd, and unknown bird, but he was able to fly. He flew back to the King's Palace and landed on one of the walls. He sang several songs until he caught the attention of the King and his people. No one could make out what the strange bird was. The people pleaded with the King to send for Wiserthanking to come to identify the bird. The King replied that he sent him to the Grim Reaper, where he would never come back. Wiserthanking, who was this strange bird, heard everything and understood why the King sent him to the Grim Reaper. The strange bird flew away, took off all the feathers, and as Wiserthan king, went to Mr. Death. He got Mr. Death to build him day and night, and brought it back to the King.

The King was amazed and tong-tired. He then proclaimed the young man to be indeed Wiserthanking. From that day on, the King allowed parents to name their children after the day they were born. Hence, since I was born on Kuda, may name was Kwaku. All people, great or small, used the names their parents gave them when they were babies. The King's knowledge and actions could not encompass everything.

Obedience to Parents is Prerequisite to a Successful Life

Listen to a tale!

We are ready for a tale!

This tale is about a King and his young Prince. Once upon a time there lived a young Prince who did evil things and obeyed nobody. He accorded no one an honor because he believed that as a Prince, it was beneath him to do so. The King pleaded with him to desist from his evil ways to no avail. His mother, the Queen, took him to his uncles (her brothers), hoping that their counsels would change his heart. But the Prince refused to change.

The young Prince's misbehaviors were source of shame for his family. His arrogance and insults were concerns of the whole nation. Finally the prince committed some criminal acts that lead the King to proclaim that he be put to death. The King was exhausted and did not know what else to do.

It was at this point that the Prince began to think of his life, his misbehaviors and disobedience. The Prince cried and begged his father to save him but the King refused. The King ordered the Prince to be brought to his presence. Upon the Prince arrival, his father gave him a critical test: a small glass filled to the brim with red wine. He was requested to carry the challenge along the wide avenue through the market full of people, and cross town, and to bring it back without spilling a drop of wine.

It was encumbered upon the Prince to take care of the wine with no spills. The chief executioner took an oath to follow the Prince. Whenever and wherever a drop of the wine fell to the ground, the Prince should be put to death there. The Prince accepted the challenge, took the full wine glass, and set out through the market to the far end of town.

After two hours, the Prince came back. He walked very slowly with the full knowledge that his life was in his own hand. The glass was full, not a drop fell down. Then the father asked him, "son, what kind of wine were they selling at the market today? Did you see your friends at the dance by the edge of town?" The young Prince replied, "I did not see anything or anybody. How could I look at somewhere else, when my whole life was at the tip of my fingers?"

The father then said, "yes, so it was. Let your life be at the end of your hands from today. Keep your eyes off temptations and evil friends and God will bless your, repent in all your ways, keep away from evil acts, and you will have a new life. Keep these advice in you heart and you too will be a pride to your parents."

The other day I was helping my grandfather with household chore and he spun this tale. Meditate on it and take a lesson from it.

The Consequences of Envy

Are you ready for a tale?

We are dying to hear a tale!

Long long ago, in a far away city, a man and his first wife had three children, two boys and a girl. He and his current wife had a girl. The ex-wife and her children lived only three blocks away, hence the children were able to be at their father's house every day. When very young the children played with their half-sibling in and around the big house all day. When they grew bigger, they played farther in the field, traveled through the woods, and to a nearby river. There they played along the bank and even swam in the river. There was a fruit bearing tree at the other side of the river. The kids called the tree Giant. They would walk across the river to climb the tree and pick its fruits to eat.

Their younger sister by the current wife could not climb the tree. The three older siblings would gladly climb, pick, and bring down the fruits for all of then to enjoy. One day their mother asked them not to pick the fruits for their younger sibling, any more.

The bigger kids obeyed their mother who was jealous of the current wife and her daughter. However, the little girl found one fruit that fell under the tree. There was a heavy rain that day and the children huddled under the tree. When they were ready to go home, they found the river was in flood. The three bigger kids easily swam across the river. But the little girl could not swim, she began to walk across as she always did. Half-way across, she could no longer walk, she could not go forward, and she could not go back. Her three siblings ran home to tell their father who ran to the river.

At the river, the father saw the little girl in the middle of the river, singing: "Giant, I picked only one, please let me go. I can't get to the bank of the river, please let me go."

Her father jumped into the river and swam very hard towards her. Her head began to bob up and down the water. Her father reached out to grab her. But he was able to grab only her hair. The lock of hair snapped, and the father was left holding the lock in his hand. The little girl disappeared under the water. Her father swam, dived to the bottom of the river, down the river, along the two banks, to no avail.

The father brought home the lock of hair. A few days later, they came to realization that she was dead and would not be seen any more. Her funeral was conducted amid grief and sorrow.

One evening, after three years, a strange bird perched on a tree branch near the house. The bird sang a song, saying:

Your beautiful daughter is coming

She is coming in splendor

She is coming

She is coming

The people could not comprehend what the bird was singing about. But Lo and behold, the lost daughter appeared. She wore rich clothes, dazzling jewelry, and with servants carrying several expensive boxes. The family and the town folk all gathered to welcome her. The following was the narrative of her adventures.

"Three years ago when I sank to the bottom of the river, I arrived in a strange city. The first person I saw was an old grandmother. The ancient one (grandmother), was sitting in the middle of her parlor. She took off her own head from her neck and put it on her lap. She was going through the hair, separating the grey hair from the black hair. The moment she heard my food steps, she put the head back on her neck, and demanded to know what I saw. I told her that I saw nothing, and that I was a stranger from a far away land. She welcomed me enthusiastically and asked me to lodge with her, and be her servant.

Three years I stayed with her, and at the end of the third year, she took me to a room that I had never been before. She said, for serving and helping her, I should look at the boxes in the room and pick whichever I fancy. I opened my eyes wide and saw several boxes, some were very bright, some were dazzling with gold, and some were just ordinary and dirty.

I picked one of the ordinary looking boxes and the old lady added nine similar looking boxes to it. She called servants to carry the boxes and set me on the journey out of the river. Now the carriers with me were going back to their home."

The little girl hardly finished the last sentence when the carriers disappeared. Then the family spread out the luggage and opened them. What they saw were astonishing: gold, expensive clothes and shoes, gold and diamond jewelry, costly beads and handkerchiefs, and so many other expensive personal items. She gave some of these things to her family, and distributed the rest among the town folk.

The news of splendor and generosity spread far and wide. However, it made the step mother more jealous and more envious. Even though she and her children were bestowed with the generosity, she wanted more. She asked her children to go back to the other bank of the river to pick the fruits. She also instructed the daughter, the youngest, not to cross the river while coming back. In that way, she told her, she too would come back home rich and famous.

The children went, as they were instructed, and the girl refused to cross the river. The river did not want to drown her, it was she who refused to cross the river, and she was drowned. She too fell to the bottom of the river and into the strange city. The first person she saw was the old lady with her own head on her lap. She was sorting the grey hair from the black hair. The ancient one put the head back on her neck and asked the girl what she saw.. She replied that she saw a very strange thing, that the old lady took off her own head and put it on her lap. And that she was sorting the grey hair from the black ones.

This second girl too was asked to stay and serve the ancient one. At the end of one year, the girl was taken to the same room and asked to pick whatever box she loved. The girl looked through the room with excitement and covetously pointed at the golden boxes. The box she picked, along with four other golden boxes were given to her. Carriers were gathered and she was set back home. The carriers brought her to the bank of the river and left.

Again the tell-tale strange bird perched on a tree branch and began to sing:

> *Your beautiful daughter is coming*
> *She is coming with foreboding news*
> *Snakes are coming, lizard s are coming*
> *Frogs are coming*

Her mother and brothers did not wait to check the meaning of the song, rather they ran to the bank of the river. There along the bank, were the dazzling golden boxes and their sister. The boxes were radiant, you couldn't look at them. They carried the boxes and with their sister returned home.

On arrival, they went straight to their house and closed the gate. Immediately the boxes were opened. Viola! Brother, come and see! The boxes were filled with snakes, lizards and frogs. The creatures began to come out, and the snakes began to bite them. The family cried out and called out for help. Eventually, the town folk broke the gate and tore down the door. Brother! It was, "run for your life," the people scrammed and scattered. The snakes, lizards, and frogs came out of the house, through the gate, into the city and spread around the world.

Brother! See what excessive envy and wanton desire led to. They brought these creatures into the world, otherwise they would have remained at the bottom of the river where they belonged

This is a nursery story my son's baby sitter scared me with the other day. May you too take a lesson from it.

The Lion and the Ground Squirrel

Here is a tale!

Let us hear a tale!

This tale moved hazardously and landed on the Lion and the Ground Squirrel.

The Lion and the Squirrel were friends who lived in a cottage upon a time. Every morning each of the friends went about his duty, worked very hard and contributed to build the friendship.

The Lion went to catch his prey, and the Squirrel went to people's farm to collect (steal) peanuts, fruits, and roots that he brought back to the cottage. The prey brought by the Lion and the roots brought by the Squirrel made a rousing meal for the two.

One afternoon, after cooking and eating delicious

meal, the two friends sat down to a lively conversation. The Squirrel asked the Lion whether he knew where the peanuts, fruits, and roots came from. The Lion said no, he did not know. The Squirrel said he got them from his uncle. He added that any time he went to help his uncle on the farm, the uncle would let him bring the goods home.

The Lion demanded to know the uncle's name. The Squirrel said his uncle was a man (human being), and that he was so strong he feared nothing; and nobody over came his power. The Squirrel added that whenever he went to see his uncle, he would knock at the door several times, and holler loud, saying "uncle, it is me, it is me," before entering the house. He never surprised his uncle. The Lion asked, "even I the Lion, the man won't fear me?"

The Squirrel said nothing scared his uncle. This infuriated the Lion, and he said to the Squirrel, "quick, let us go to see your uncle, so I the Lion will get to know him." The Squirrel did not like the proposal but the Lion insisted. The Squirrel replied. "look, my friend, it is not a joke, it is true, nothing scare my uncle. Let us live, and leave him alone." The Lion commanded, "stand up, let's go."

The Lion's boasting was that he was the King of the Jungle, and no one else could have power greater than he. He could not stand such an idea.

After a long discussion, the Squirrel agreed to go with

his friend to see his uncle. They set out on the journey in the afternoon. After a while the Squirrel told his friend, "let us wait here." They waited and hid among the bushes where they could clearly see the road. Soon the pair saw a woman and her daughter, with loads balancing on their heads, coming towards them. When mother and daughter reached them, the Lion wanted to jump on them. The Squirrel stopped him by saying those were not his uncle.

About an hour later, the uncle appeared, striding confidently and fearlessly down the road. On his shoulder was a loaded gun, and around his waste, was a belt full of ammunition. The Squirrel informed his friend that was his uncle on the way coming. When the uncle reached the pair, the Squirrel crossed the road, disappearing among the bushes. The Lion, fearless and showing his strength, roared, and roared, and jumped into the middle of the road. Hi mien stood up, he was an awesome sight to see.

Just as the Lion Jumped into the road, "pawoo ooo!" the gun reported. But the Lion very much wanted to show his strength and energy, would not run away. He shuttled towards the man. There upon, the man reached into his belt and pulled out daggers, and threw two of then at the Lion. The Lion's face was a mesh, his mien a bloody mesh too. The all powerful Lion was warbling in blood. The mighty King of the jungle staggered and ran to the cottage. The wise Squirrel was standing in the middle of the cottage when the humbled Lion appeared. The Lion was bleeding all over, and loosing strength.

The Squirrel was aware that the man would come to the cottage soon. The Lion's trail of blood became a high way for the man to follow. The Squirrel told the Lion that since his body was all bloody, he the Squirrel would go fetch water to clean him. The Lion agreed. The wise Squirrel again ran away from the Lion. Not long after, the man could be seen at the edge of the cottage. The Lion, in pain, was lying under a tree. Without hesitation, "pawo oo," the gun reported again. The mighty Lion shook but could not stand up, his jaws clang, and no more roar or sound came out of him.

The mighty and powerful should stoop to conquer. Boasting of strength leads to downfall. "Verily," said the Squirrel, "life is not a question of strength and energy but wisdom and agility."

The Alligator and the Boar (Pig)

Are you ready for a tale?

A tale is long overdue!

This tale moved in a zigzag and landed on the alligator and the boar.

One day the boar was roaming around looking for his daily food. He came to the bank of a river. When he raised his head up and looked at the surface of the river, he saw a big alligator sunning himself on a flat broad stone in the middle of the river. Instantly the alligator too saw the boar. The boar was on a bluff and had to climb down to the edge of the water. He climbed down a little, stopped, and greeted the alligator. The alligator replied by smashing his tail on the water, "Buu! Buu! Buu!"

The alligator said, "our meeting today calls for a contest,

to see who is stronger than the other." The boar replied, "that is exactly my wish." The boar turned round, looked for a big stone, picked it up, and threw it at the alligator. The stone pinned the alligator down. It took a while before the alligator freed himself from under the stone. When he finally came out of the state of unconsciousness, the gator proclaimed, "I am the King of all river animals, nothing overcomes me."

The alligator gathered all the water in his pouch, and hauled it at the boar. The water hit him, rolled him over, and sent him very far away. The boar lost consciousness for a while but when he came to, he went back to the river bank. The boar praised the alligator by saying, "it is obvious you are very strong, climb up the bank to where I am and let us fight."

The gator replied, "come down half way and I will climb up half way to meet you." The combatants did as they requested. They came close to each other and ready themselves for a combat. The boar sank his canine teeth into the soft belly of the gator, and held on to it. The gator grabbed the boar's throat with is paws, and held on to it. They engaged in this mortal embrace till both died, since none of them was stronger than the other.

The wise man said, "unrestrained aggression leads to destruction." This was a story I heard at the bull session the other day, and I passed it on to you.

The Wretched Who Became Rich Then Lost It All

Listen to a tale!

Tell us a tale!

This tale was about a wretched man. This wretched man became so poor that his clothes were all in rags. He used the bark of trees to wrap around himself. He slept on palm leaves for he had no bed. He used broken pots for cooking, and broken plates to serve his meals. Because of his deplorable state, he was always talking about his misery and also about God, that God did not create him well.

Dear friend, wait on the Lord and everything will be alright. The constant crying over his misery and the negative thoughts about God finally reached God. One early morning when the wretched man woke up he saw a chain ladder descending from Heaven to the front door of his tattered house. He heard a voice from Heaven asking him to climb the chain ladder up to Heaven. He was amazed at the request, however, he quickly climbed the chain ladder. Soon he was in the presence of God. God demanded to know why the miserable man was always calling on Him, and petitioning Him. The poor wretched fellow could not give any answer. God told him that he was created very well but because he did not take care of himself, he became miserable.

However, the disastrous state of the wretched man led God to have mercy on him, and blessed him one more time. He was given a chest of gold to take back to earth to use any way he pleased. There was one stipulation attached to the gift: the man was never to ride in a palanquin. Kings were carried from place to place in palanquins, in those days.

The wretched man became very rich indeed. He had multitude of possessions and was in no need of anything. His fame, riches, and generosity spread all over the land. One day this rich man took account of his riches and possessions, and found them to be good. There was only one thing in the world he did not have. He had no palanquin. He envied Kings, for they were carried around in palanquins. So the rich man bought a palanquin. People thought of him and talked about him as a King, for he behaved like a King. He gave orders to his followers that they should not carry him in the palanquin. They should carry the empty palanquin in front of him, while he walked behind the palanquin.

A great many years later, the rich man took another account of his possessions, and found them to be good. He even had a palanquin. But there was one thing in the world he did not do. He did not ride in the palanquin. Dear friend, the rich man, in his pride, forgot the law given to him by God. One day the rich man called some strongest of his workers and asked them to get ready for a task. The rich man got ready too. He put on the best of his costumes, gold and silver jewelry, diamond rings, shoes, etc. He asked the strongest men to bring out the palanquin. They did. The rich man got into the palanquin. Just as he was about to sit down and give command to be carried around like a King, the RETINUE disappeared. His costumes, jewelry, and shoes also disappeared. His riches and possessions all gone. All were immediately lost. In this way the rich man became the poorest of the wretched.

This was what the elders told us at public square gathering, and I want to pass it on to you. Those with ears to hear, let them hear!

The Rabbit and the Wiseman

In the mood for a tale?

We are dying to hear a tale!

This tale involved the Rabbit and the Wiseman.

One day the Rabbit was roaming round the country side and came across a very Wiseman. The Rabbit asked the Wiseman to make him wise because he, the Rabbit, was not smart or wise. The Wiseman agreed. He gave the Rabbit a gourd (bottle), calabash, and a straight long stick. The Rabbit was asked to go and fill the gourd with birds, fill the calabash with the milk of a deer, and to rope a live snake on the straight stick. All these things had to be brought back to the Wiseman.

They would be used in making the Rabbit wise. The Rabbit agreed, picked the items and set out on a journey.

He came to the bank of a river and sat down to rest.

It wasn't long, when two birds came to the river to drink. The Rabbit jumped high and fell to the ground and began rolling. The birds demanded to know what was the matter with the Rabbit. He answered them saying he heard people argued that birds could not fill this gourd. So he had a bet with them that birds could fill the gourd.

The birds told him to be patient, wait and see what would happen. The birds went to bring other birds and they filled the gourd. Immediately the Rabbit put the lid on the mouth of the gourd and closed it tight. Then he sat down again by the river bank to wait. After a while the deer came to drink. The Rabbit went through the same routine to attract the deer's attention. The deer wanted to know what was wrong with the Rabbit. The Rabbit replied that people were betting that the deer could not fill the calabash with her milk. He the Rabbit too believed the deer could not do it. The deer told him to wait to see a miracle. The deer took her time and filled the calabash with her milk. Then the deer drank the water from the river and went her way.

The Rabbit remained at the same place, happy to over come the first two challenges. He was also thinking about where to get a snake. Suddenly, a long snake came by the river to drink. The Rabbit repeated his traumatic behavior, and the snake asked what was the matter with him. The Rabbit replied that he heard people arguing that the snake could not be as long as this stick. The Rabbit put the stick on the ground to see if the snake measured up to it. Immediately the Rabbit roped the snake to the stick in four different places. The snake was alive but could not writhe or struggle itself out of the roping.

The Rabbit brought the various things to the Wiseman, so as to be made wise. The Wiseman was surprised to see the Rabbit's accomplishment. He asked the Rabbit how he managed to get a snake that was not easy to catch, birds that flew high in the sky, and milk from a deer that usually ran away from people. The Wiseman said to obtain all these things was a miracle as well as a display of Knowledge. And that there was no more any Knowledge or Wisdom that the Rabbit did not possess.

The Rabbit went home very happy and very proud. From that day till this day people praised the Rabbit and said he was Wiser than most Wild animals.

This was what the elders initiated me with. Think about it, and apply your Knowledge.

Vilifying and Slander of Women

Are you ready for a tale?

A tale must be told!

A great many years ago, this tale was circulated, defaming, vilifying, and slandering women. This is the gist of the story.

A man took a woman for a wife, but he was dirt poor. He worked hard and hustled around for their daily bread. The family became wretched, but his wife did not leave him. On the contrary, the two entered into an agreement that even death would not separate them. They lived for many years and their love for each other was admired by everybody.

One day the wife become suddenly ill and died. The town folks came to the funeral, contributed money to buy a casket. The funeral service was held at the local church. After the service they headed toward the cemetery for burial. The last RITES were conducted by the grave side. However, just when they were about to lower the casket, the man jumped into the grave. The people had never heard of such a thing, so they asked him to come out. But the man refused, explaining to the town folks that he and his wife had agreed that if one died, the other should be also buried along. In that way, even death would not set them apart.

The people were perplexed but were not ready to bury a life person. They went home, leaving the casket with the dead wife in it, by the grave. The husband remained inside the grave. He refused to sleep. Since he could not bury himself and the wife together, he remained there, guarding the coffin.

On the fourth night, he felt into a deep sleep. In a dream he saw a man standing by him. The stranger asked him what he was doing there among the dead. He told the husband to go home to mourn the wife. But the husband refused . The stranger asked for explanation. The husband explained the agreement between him and his wife. The stranger told the husband that the dead were no longer aware of anything. Thinking and repentance did not exist among the dead. Since those things were not possible, he would revive the wife for him to take home to continue their love. The stranger asked him whether he was sure the wife loved him. The husband said indeed they loved each other and there was no lie between them.

The stranger prayed by the coffin. The wife who had been dead since four days, woke up. The stranger handed the wife to the husband and said the love was indeed a true love, not false. They thanked the stranger and went home. Their love for each other grew even stronger. The town folks admired them. However, they were still poor and wretched as ever. The husband continued to work at odd jobs for their living.

Many years later, the husband went far from home to take odd jobs. He was gone just a few days when a splendidly dressed man on a white horse appeared before the wife. The stranger was obviously rich. He handed the woman several expensive gifts, informing her that he wanted to marry her. The woman did not agree to this proposal. The stranger insisted that she accept the gifts and marry him. The woman was enchanted with the expensive gifts. She told the stranger that the only way he could marry her was to take her away from the town to a far away land. The stranger agreed and they left town together.

After a few days of travel, they realized they had indeed left her home town and were together. At a bend in the road, they met the husband who was returning home. The husband demanded to know where the stranger was taking his wife. The stranger replied that the woman was not the poor man's wife. The woman also stated that she was not the wife of the wretched fellow, more over, she did not know him.

The two men began to fight over the woman. While they were fighting, the horse rider asked the woman to hand him a dagger to plunge into the husband. If he died they would be free to go on their way. The woman reached for the dagger and handed it to the stranger. As the stranger received the dagger, he asked the man and the woman whether they recognized him. Immediately the stranger changed, and they recognized him to be the fellow who revived the woman from the dead, by the grave. The stranger took the hand of the wife and handed it to the husband, and said, "I am not taking your wife from you. I am testing your love for her. Take her home and continue to marry her, if you can."

Now, here is a question for you and me. If you were the husband, would you continue to marry the woman, and you woman, would you continue to follow this wretched husband.

If you know a story to defame, slander, and vilify men, tell it to whomever will listen.

The King
and the Innocent Youngman

In the mood for a tale?

May a tale be told!

This tale staggered out of the blue sky and landed on a man, his wife, their son, the King and the Queen.

In the days of yore a man and his wife had a son. The son was a paragon of handsomeness. The parents loved him very much but did not want anybody to see or talk to him. Afraid that others might love him to death they kept him within the homestead, and locked the gate. When he was four years old and roaming round the yard, they provided him with a bow and arrow. He used the tools to shoot birds around their cottage.

One day when the parents were visiting relatives, the Youngman, now about 18 years old, brought out the bow and arrow as he always did. He followed the birds along the creek to the edge of the cottage. He shot at a bird, missed it, but the arrow landed on the other side of the fence, right into the bath house of the King's wife, the Queen! But the worse misfortune was that the Queen was taking her bath at that time. When the Queen saw the arrow, she looked over the edge of the fence to see who was shooting. She saw the Youngman, of striking handsomeness holding a bow, and looking at her. She had never seen or heard about this singularly striking handsome Youngman.

The Queen asked the Youngman to climb over the fence, enter the bath, and retrieve his arrow. But the Youngman refused. He stood there, thinking how to get his arrow back. After a while the Queen finished her bath, put on her clothes, and invited the Youngman to follow her into the palace, to retrieve the arrow. He followed her into the palace. At the palace, the Queen inquired about him, about his parents, their names and their abode. When the Youngman felt a little at ease about the new surrounding, for he had never seen a palace before, the Queen demanded the Youngman have a knowledge of her. The Youngman refused.

The King was home that day but unaware of the goings on in the Queen's quarters. The King brought out his valuables to air and sun, a routine act. Among the valuables were cloaks, regal uniforms, and jewelry. The Queen was asked to look after the garments and to bring them inside when it started to rain. The King left the palace for the nearby plantation and stables. The Youngman managed to run out of the palace. He got home before the parents returned. Meanwhile the rains came, very heavy, with gusting winds. The Queen, in her lust for the Youngman, did not remember to bring the sunning garments inside during the rains. The garments were floated away and the jewelry were guttered away.

On his way back to the palace, the King met his valuables in the torrential gutter. He picked them and brought them home. At the Queen's quarters, he saw the Queen sitting on a lazy sofa, smoking a pipe. The King asked her where she had been when the torrential rains came and floated away the valuables. The Queen did not reply. The King asked the question second time. The Queen interjected, "are you ENCHANTING GOLD or what?" The Youngman's name was ENCHANTING GOLD. He was given this name because of his perfection.

The King was astonished, he had never heard such a name in his Kingdom. All birth registrations were in his palace, but ENCHANTING GOLD was not among them. The King issued orders that all young men should be brought to the public square within the palace to be examined. But ENCHANATING GOLD was not among them The King asked the Queen whether the young man she was enchanted with was among them. The Queen said no. The King issued orders again to his messengers to search homes and rooms till such a young man was found. This time, the messengers did find ENCHANTING GOLD. Brother, if you too saw him, you would know you have met enchantment. Truly, his look, manners, the expensive clothes and jewelry the parents put on him were things to admire and gawk at. The Youngman was shining and dazzling as a newly minted gold. The moment the queen saw him coming, she stood up and yield, "now he is coming."

His parents were carrying a throne and a footstool. At the square, they set the throne and the footstool down. He sat on the throne and put his feet on the soft dazzling pillow. The King asked his wife if this was the young man. She replied in affirmative, with a smirk of smile and taunting laughter at the King. The crowd applauded happily in admiration, in that they had never seen such a surpassed handsomeness in their city.

The King demanded to know what was between the Youngman and his wife. The Youngman replied that there was nothing between them. The Queen was asked the same question. She replied, "yes, when you, my King, left for the plantation, this Youngman broke into my bedroom and raped me." The question was returned to the Youngman who said again that there was nothing between them. The King rose from his throne, and said he was happy to see such a Youngman in his Kingdom. If he the King were a woman, she would want to marry the Youngman. The King proclaimed the Youngman faultless and asked him to go home.

The Queen, then rose from her seat, and disagreed with the King. The Queen said the Youngman must be put through an ordeal to ascertain his innocence before she would be satisfied. The King disagreed but the Queen insisted. Eventually the King relented. On the way to the ordeal, his father gave him a small nut to keep in his mouth. The ordeal was a tall palmetto tree with sharp stakes pointing upwards and anchored firmly around the tree. The Youngman was asked to climb the palmetto tree up to the leaves, and while there to let go himself, if he landed on the sharp stakes and not hurt he was to repeat the motion seven times. After that, his innocence would be established. Palmetto tree was monolithic, had no branches, the leaves so pliable that they could not even hold small bird.

The Youngman climbed the tree. At the top he let go himself. But just before he landed, the stakes turned themselves downwards, and he was not hurt. He climbed six

times and six times in wonder, the stakes turned themselves. The King then said enough was enough but the
Queen insisted that he climb the seventh time. Just before
he began the seventh climb, he took out the nut from his
mouth and gave it to his father. He bade them good bye
and said he would not come back. In a happy, blissful
mood, with a song on his lips, he climbed to the top, and
let go. Immediately there was thunder and lightening, a
dazzling display of fire works in the sky. The Youngman
disappeared in the clouds. The multitude stood there in
awe and in wonderment, looking up into the sky and into
the clouds.

To this day, it is said, whenever thunder and lightening
occur, it is the Youngman meeting and greeting his parents.

This was the nursery tale my grandfather comforted me
with the other day, and I passed it on to you. May you take
a lesson from it.

No Matter What the Secret, Somebody Knows

Here is a plain, old tale!

May we hear a plain, old tale!

Back in the days of tabloid newspapers, journals, televisions, radios, and gossiping, nothing was kept secret. Everything was exposed, including the innuendoes, lies, and half truths. No secret could be kept anywhere.

One fellow had a secret. He was determined to keep it to himself. He tried to hide it in the house, under the bed, at the work place and so forth, but people were at all these places. However, nobody appeared to know the secret, and nobody was talking or writing about it. He had to hide it before it was found out. So one day he decided to take the secret far away into the forest. There he would bury it and nobody would know. It took him two whole days of walk to get to the primeval forest. Nobody ever visited there, and nobody was around nor followed him. He dug a big deep hole, buried the secret, covered it with soil and scattered leaves over the soil.

He retraced his footsteps back to town. At the edge of the town he met a few people talking about the secret, the one he had buried. By the time he got to the town square, almost everybody was talking about that particular secret.

Somebody knew that secret. Who was that body?

The Consequences of Disobedience

Here is the tale begging to be told!

By all means, tell us the tale!

This legend has to do with a young man not taking the advice given by his parents and others.

Not long ago, on a distant shore, a young man and a young woman fell in love. Their love for each other was so strong they agreed to get marry after graduating from College. Their wishes were fulfilled. They graduated, the young man with a degree in Accounting and the young woman with a degree in medicine. The doctor went into private practice and became successful in a short time. She was helping the young man financially while he was looking for a job. They joined a local church. Their strong love led to marriage with a big ceremony at the church. At last the young man got a job at the local bank. His hard work led to a quick promotion as the branch manager

After a few years the couple were blessed with four children. The home office (headquarters) of the local bank was in America. One day a request came from the home office asking the local director to send some one to America for further studies. The director and his co-workers agreed that the young man should be the one to go to America. He went home to tell his wife, the children, and his parents. However, he was inclined not to go because of his family. But the family encouraged him to accept the honor and to go for further studies.

The day of departure came. He was ready to set out on the journey. His parents, church members, and the pastor gave him sound advice. Among other things, he was advised not to carry on affairs with women while in America. Such acts would lead to his neglecting his wife and children back home. All the people accompanied him to the airport from where he flew away to America. He was warmly received on arrival. This calmed his anxieties during orientation. He was not the only foreigner at the graduate school. Men and women, from all over the world, came to the school. They were young, handsome and beautiful bunch. Even though he studied along the most attractive women, he kept the advice given him at home. He was ambitious and courageous.

The young man was steadfast and courageous for two years. Then he met the most beautiful thing from Australia. They became fast friends, called each other, and did things he was warned not to do. Not long, he left this young woman for another one. He became a playboy. His love affairs and parties began to interfere with his studies. He could not graduate. The graduate school and the home bank asked him to return home.

He went back home without a degree and in shame. He lost his old job at the local bank. His wife took the children and left him, she had heard of his affairs in America. It was a triple misfortune, he left the women in America, lost his family at home and became unemployed. Since he did not listen to his parents, church members and the pastor, he fell into shame, poverty and disorientation.

My friend, take parental advice, think about it day and night, and better life will come your way. Now you have heard a tall story, or could it be true?

Honesty

In the mood for a story?

We are dying to hear a story!

The lesson from this story is honesty. The story moved crazily and landed on two young men who were friends in high school Their love and friendship were so strong that even water could not pass between them. They graduated with valued Diplomas. It was not long when Kwassi, the older one, got a chance to go to Europe for further studies. After graduating, he got a good paying job.

Kwassi and his friend Kwame were in constant communication. One day Kwame got a letter asking whether he had received the pocket money sent through Kwassi's parents. He replied in affirmative with thanks. Kwassi then wrote back saying he would like to build a house at home.

Upon his return the two friends with their families would live in the house. He would send the plan, requirements, and funds to Kwame to build the house. All Kwame had to do was find a contractor to do the job, and to let Kwassi know when it was completed.

Kwame agreed. The plan, the requirements for colors, furniture and furnishing were received. The funds too began to come.

Brother be honest with a friend. Kwame spent most of the funds on frivolous things. He partied, gambled and went on spending spree. Kwame built a house indeed, but cut back on the dimensions: height, width, and length. Hardly any furnishing or furniture were provided. Dear friend, if you saw the house, you would wish it had never been built. But what would you do?

Kwame wrote to his friend that the house was completed. His friend wrote back setting a date of his arrival. Kwassi returned. They picked a date for Open House, friends and relatives on both sides, along with the whole town were invited. Sumptuous banquet with drinks and music were provided. At the end of the banquet, Kwassi addressed the gathering. He called on Kwame to let him know that their friendship would be for ever. He was not going to be living in their home town, so he wanted to leave Kwame a token of their friendship: The House. Indeed, he said, the house was built for Kwame. Kwassi thanked his friend for a job well done.

Kwame covered his face with hands and buried his head between his knees in shame. He remembered all he did, how he wasted the money, and put up a shoddy building. Kwame thought he was cheating his friend when in fact he was building a faulty house for himself.

The philosopher says be true to yourself, be honest at all times, and better things will come your way. I heard this story from my grandfather, may it be of a lesson to you.

Origins of Songs, Dances, and Plays: The Theater

Here is everlasting tale!

We are ever ready for a tale!

In ancient times human beings did not know how to sing, dance or play. They lived in towns, villages and cottages. They farmed the land, fished in the rivers and lakes, and hunted in the woods.

One day a hunter went hunting in the primeval forest. He had traversed the forest for a long while but did not find any animal to shoot with his bow and arrow. Eventually he arrived at a clearing that was swept clean but empty. In the middle of the clearing was a big soaring tree with many branches and dark broad leaves. Since he saw nobody nor heard any sound, he hid behind the bushes waiting to find out what went on there.

It was not long when chairs began falling from the branches, and arranged themselves in a neat manner around the big tree. After the arrangement forest animals began arriving one after the other. They came in large numbers. One of the animals had child in hand.

When the last one arrived, they began to sing several songs. While singing, those sitting down tossed the child from one to the other around the circle. Others within the circle were engaged in furious gyrations to unknown rhythms. The hunter was amazed. He had never heard songs, seen dancing nor plays. He hid there quietly in wonderment.

In the afternoon it appeared the animals were tired and the activities were slacking. Barrels of wine were brought out from under a nearby tree. The animals drank the wine, got drunk. The whole festival started all over again. The songs became more hilarious, the dancing more complex, and the plays more serious.

Late in the evening the activities came to a lingering end. All the animals left. The chairs returned themselves to the branches. The hunter who had carefully listened to the songs, and keenly observed the plays as well as the dancing, retraced his footsteps back home. At home, he told the story, taught the songs, dances and plays to human beings. The people loved the activities.

That was how singing, dancing, and playing came to be among human beings. The other day my grandmother kidded me with this story, now may I pass it on to you. Listen and make a story of your own.

The Eagle, the Turtle, and the Big Flat Stone

Here is a tale!

We are dying to hear a tale!

Here is a tale about disastrous end of envy. Once upon a time the Turtle had smooth cloak of arms around his body. Other animals commented on the beauty of his shells and how strong they were. However, Mr. Turtle envied the birds. Birds flew high up in the sky and to many places of their choice, in a short time. Mr. Turtle wanted to fly like birds. So one day he went to the Eagle and asked him to teach him how to fly. The Eagle was one of the largest birds and also King of the birds.

The Eagle told Mr. Turtle, "look my friend, you are asking for something you are not made to do. How can you fly since you do not have any feathers? Your request is ridiculous in that no part of your body is made to fly." The more the Eagle tried to dissuade (stop) Mr. Turtle, the more Mr. Turtle begged to be taught to fly. Finally when the Eagle was exhausted in preventing Mr. Turtle to fly, he agreed to teach him. The Eagle asked Mr. Turtle to come near him.

Suddenly the Eagle grasped Mr. Turtle with his clauses and flew high up in the sky. When they were very high in the sky, the Eagle informed Mr. Turtle that the only way he could learn to fly was to let him go, and fly on his own. Mr. Turtle being very happy to be up there with the birds, and believing he was flying on his own, gladly agreed. The Eagle let go Mr. Turtle. Mr. Turtle who could not fly fell, tumbling all the way from the sky and landed on a Big Flat Stone.

Mr. Turtle broke in pieces, his once proud smooth shells were shattered all over the place. The Ants and Mites in that land had a meeting over Mr. Turtle's fate. They pitied him, and decided to help him. They put the shattered shells together, sewed them, and put the new crumbled, zig-zagged shells on Mr. Turtle. The Ants and the Mites were too small to see the whole of Mr. Turtle, however, their handy work is what you see on Mr. Turtle today.

Friends, be proud of your natural endowments and accept them. May this tale sink into your ears.

Patience and Wisdom

Here is a wise tale!

May a wise tale be told!

This tale landed on the King of all animals and on the turtle. Not long ago, the King wanted to find a husband for his daughter. The daughter was the most beautiful girl in the Kingdom. The King called all the eligible bachelors and told them that his daughter was ready to marry. However, she would marry the first man that brought him bales of thatch. Thatch was used for roofing in that Kingdom. All the bachelors agreed and set out to make thatch. The turtle also saw the beautiful girl and longed in his heart to marry her. But the turtle knew he could not compete with the other animals in haste and quickness in bringing the thatch to the King.

So the turtle went out and constructed a drum. The drum was sonorous and clear in sound. The turtle set out on the path that everybody took to get bales of thatch. He soon realized that some of the animals by-passed him and some were already returning with their bales. Since the turtle did not want anybody to beat him in the trial for first place, he began drumming and singing. The drumming was rhythmical and the song was very sweet saying: "it is to the turtle that everybody is coming." When the other animals heard the drumming and the song they began to laugh and to dance. They unloaded their bales of thatch at the feet of the turtle, and danced away. Soon they forgot everything about the bales of thatch and danced non-stop backward to the field.

The turtle was patient and took his time. While still drumming and singing, he managed to gather as much bales as he could carry, and set out homeward. Every now and then he looked back and if the others were too close he would beat the drum and sing the song. With this wise trick he was the first to reach the palace with bales of thatch.

The news spread all over the Kingdom that the turtle was the first in bringing bales of thatch. What did the King do? He gave his beautiful daughter to the turtle to marry. Why did the turtle marry this girl? It was his patience as well as his wisdom. Go and be wise!

The Dog, the Chameleon, and the Throne

In the mood for a tale?

We are ready for a tale!

This tale involved the dog, the chameleon, and the throne. One day the elephant who was then King of all animals realized he was rich, had everything, but no child. The King had no child to bequeath his earthly possessions. The King called for the gathering of all animals and spoke to them. He said, "I am old and in my final days. You have listened to me and served me sincerely. I would like to reward each and every one of you by distributing my possessions."

In those ancient days the animals did not have all their body parts. Some were missing an ear, an eye, an arm or a leg. Others had no mouth, no nose or feet. Still some had no tails or manes. The King took accounts of all the missing parts and set a date for distributing them to each animal. The festival date arrived and during the celebration the King distributed the missing parts. Every animal became whole. They were all very happy.

Toward the end of the celebration the King said there was one thing left to give away. It was his throne, he did not know which animal to give it to, hence he left the throne in nearby city. Whoever ran there first and sat on the throne would have it. The time came and all the animals lined up. The signal was given and each one began to run. They all ran hard but the dog ran faster. The dog, proud of his strength and quickness, told the others not to bother to run for he would be there first, and the throne would be his. The dog continued to run very fast, leaving the others behind.

About an hour later, the dog looked back, did not see anyone. He was exhausted, laid down to rest, and fell asleep. Meanwhile the chameleon running by, saw the dog and attached himself to the dog's tail. The sound and noise of the approaching animals woke the dog up. He set out again to run faster than the others. Of course, he was unaware of the chameleon holding on to his tail. The dog arrived in the nearby city and at the throne. He looked around, did not see anyone, looked at the throne, nobody was sitting on it. But when the dog tried to get on the throne, the chameleon let go the dog's tail and sat on the throne first. The chameleon also shouted, "do not sit on me, I am on the throne."

If you were there you would not believe it. The situation was tense, and not easy for the dog. He became very angry and wanted to throw the chameleon off the throne. The other animals had arrived to see what was going on. They said they could not tell which one of the contenders arrived first. Therefore they requested the dog and the chameleon to walk in front of them. Whoever walked like a King would have the throne.

The dog could not believe in this very easy solution, he knew he could beat the chameleon in walking. So the dog walked fast right past the animals. Then it was the turn of Mr. Chameleon to walk. He stood up, looked at the assembled masses of animals, and picked the first step, He began to walk slowly with gaiety. To make a step he would lift one foot up, wait a while before putting it down. Then the other foot in the same manner. All the animals shouted in happiness, "this is the King's walk, it is majestic, it is noble, it is a smooth and cultured walk. The throne belongs to Mr. Chameleon. May he be the King, may he reign over us."

From that day the Chameleon accepted the throne and reigned over the animals. He was very proud of the throne and of himself. Whenever any of his subjects visited him, the Chameleon would tell them, "I am rich and have everything, I have even the clothes or costumes you are wearing." There upon the Chameleon would change his colors to reflect the colors the visitor was wearing. Whether the colors were black, white, multi-colored, the Chameleon possessed them all. And very proud to show them off.

The race in this life is not necessarily to the fastest but to the wise, patient, and persevering.

Change Has Its Rewards

Here is a tale of Behavioral Change!

May we hear a tale of Change!

In the days of yore, there lived a man, his wife, and two young children. They lived by themselves in a cottage not too far from the village. The older child, Janet, was ten years, and the younger child, Jack, was only five years when their parents died. The two orphans remained in the cottage by themselves. This is the story of their painful journey (odyssey) through the world.

One day Janet put rice on the heath to cook, then went to the nearby creek to fetch water. On her return, she found that Jack had put several pebbles (small stones) into the rice. When Janet questioned him, he began to cry uncontrollably. Janet threw the pot of rice away, and put another food on the stove. She left again to fetch more water. On her return, she found that Jack had set the cottage on fire, everything burned down. Janet did not know what to do. There was no place to live. She picked Jack and they left the cottage. They traveled aimlessly around the country side till they came to a village.

The two lodged with an old lady who welcomed them with open arms. After a while the people got to know them and Jack played with the children. Janet felt free to go on errands, to farms, to the creek to fetch water, and to the markets in nearby towns. On her return from the market, one day, she was told that during play, Jack plugged out the eyes of the chief's son. Fearful for their lives, Janet packed their belongings and they ran away.

It was not long, when they realized they were being followed by the chief and his security guards. They ran faster and faster till they came to a big Baobab tree. They climbed the tree and hid in its big branches. Soon the chief and his retinue arrived. The pursuers were tired, and sat down under the tree to rest, unaware of the two in the branches. Jack wanted to move along the branches to be exactly above the chief, so he could pee on his head. When his sister refused, he began to cry uncontrollably. Of course, they were discovered. The pursuers began to cut down the Baobab.

Luck was on their side. A Big Bird that usually carried people from place to place was flying by. Janet begged the Bird to fly them away. The Big Bird agreed. They hopped on its wings, and the Big Bird flew away. The rule on flying Big Bird was that no one touched its tail. The impish (mischievous) Jack would not adhere to any rule. He managed to grab Big Bird's tail. There upon, the siblings fell to the ground. They set out again on their odyssey till they came to another town. Here too they were lucky and were welcomed by another old lady.

In the afternoon, they were told about the rule of the town. A curfew was on at four in the afternoon, everyone had to abide by it. A huge monster had been coming to town at night to grab people on the street and take them away. They were also told about the order of the King. Whoever succeeded in killing the monster would get half of the King's wealth, and become the chief of the town.

Jack who by then was fifteen years old, decided to repent from his mischievous ways. He would do something good for humanity. He went to the woods to cut fire woods. He made a big fire at the edge of town and began to heat seven stones in the fire. The stones were red hot when the monster appeared at night. Since Jack was still up and around the fire, the monster saw him, and ran over to grab him. When it came near, Jack picked the stones one by one and threw them at the monster. The red hot stones hit the monster and killed it.

Early next morning, Jack cut off the monster's tail and took it to the King. Jack was rewarded, and given half of the wealth of the Kingdom, and also made the chief over the town. At long last, Janet and Jack found a home. The long suffering Janet was rewarded for her patience with her impish brother. Jack's repentance (change) from evil ways was rewarded with a chiefdom.

The Consequence of Evil Response to Good Deed

Here is a twisted tale!

May we hear a twisted tale!

One day, a young man called Anani was returning home from his farm. Anani came across a very old crocodile. The croc had come too far from the river and could not walk back. He begged Anani to take him back to the river. Anani agreed, roped the croc on a stretcher (pole) and carried him to the river.

When they got to the river, Anani unloaded the crocodile, removed the rope and asked him to get into the water. Instead the crocodile grabbed Anani and said he was very hungry and would therefore eat Anani. Anani refused to be eaten. The two got into a fight. The crocodile's intent was to eat him, and Anani's intent was to wrestle himself loose, so as to escape.

Mr. Rabbit who came to the river to drink saw the antagonists. Mr. Rabbit went over to separate the two and asked why they were wrestling. Each one told his story. Mr. Rabbit said the only way he could judge the case was for the antagonists to go back to the beginning, from the place they started.

They all agreed. The crocodile was roped on a stretcher, carried by Anani back to the original place, with Mr. Rabbit in-tow. On arrival, Anani unloaded the crocodile, still roped on the stretcher. Mr. Rabbit's judgment:

Anani, kill that crocodile!

Anani complied.

Mr. Rabbit saved Anani from the evil machination of the crocodile. The crocodile met his just reward.

The Spider and His Brother-in-Law

Here is a lesson upon a tale!

May we hear a lesson upon a tale!

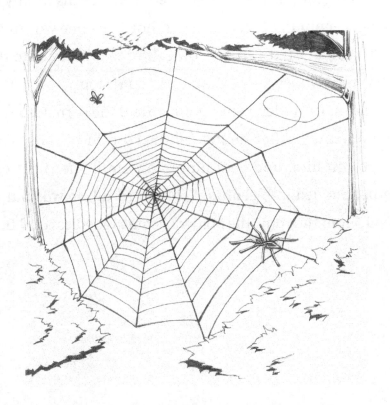

A great many years ago, a severe famine came over the land. Many people in the city died from hunger. The Spider and his family too lived in the city. Osu, Spider's brother-in-law (his wife's brother), was a hard working fellow who grew corn on a large farm. Osu's wife made brumes for sale. Hence they were well off and did not suffer from the famine.

However, Spider and his family were lazy, all day long, they did nothing. Their job was to attach themselves to corners up the walls, inside their home. Consequently they suffered from hunger. At night, Spider would go secretly into his brother-in-law's silo to steal corn for his family to live on. Eventually Osu found out that some one was stealing his corn. Osu asked the Town Crier to announce to the public that whoever was doing it should stop.

One night Spider went again to steal the corn. Osu was hiding nearby. After he loaded the corn in his bag, Osu jumped on him, and beat him to a pump. The cuts from the beating led to bleeding. Spider bled till he was out of blood. From that day, the Spider became bloodless and flat.

A Brief Tale

Folks, here is a brief tale!

We are dying to hear a short tale!

A severe famine came over a far away city. Twin brothers, Atsu and Atsuse were orphans who lived in that same city. One day, the twins set out on a journey to find a job that would help them buy food. Soon they came to a fork in the road, and had a discussion on which road to take:

Atsu: Let us go together on one road till we find a job.

Atsuse: No, each one will take a different road.

Soon, they agreed to go on their separate ways. They journeyed several days, traveled round they country side till they came back to where they parted. Atsu found a gourd and Atsuse found a small key. Immediately they used the small key to open the gourd.

Surprise! Inside the gourd was a very short tail of a mouse. If the mouse's tail was long, this tale too would be long, all the way to its end. Since the tail was short, this was the end of the tale!

Why the Rabbit was Domesticated

Here is a marvelous tale!

Let's hear a marvelous tale!

This tale fell upon the Rabbit and all animals. In ancient times all the animals lived in the jungle. Their King was the Lion. The Lion ruled supremely over the animals and all lived happily in the primeval forest. A long drought fell upon the land. The lack of rains led to lack of growth of trees, vegetations and crops. This led to lack of food and a great famine. The King called a meeting of all animals to decide what to do. At the Conference, they agreed to sell their ears to get money. The money would be used to buy tools in digging a well. The well would provide water to drink and to irrigate the crops to grow food.

The Rabbit who had the biggest and the longest ears refused to go along. All other animals went ahead, contributed their ears, sold them, made money, bought the
equipment, and dug the well. Soon the well was full of
water. The first cup of water from the well was given to the
Lion to use in prayer (Libation) to thank God for the water.

The Rabbit who refused to participate went to steal the
water. The King ordered his arrest and trial. The Rabbit
went to steal the water again, but before they could arrest
him, he ran away. The Rabbit's friend, the monkey, caught
him and brought him to the King. All animals were assembled and in their presence, the Rabbit was sentenced to
death. But before the sentence could be carried out, the
Rabbit ran away to take refuge among human beings.
From that day, the Rabbit became domesticated, he dared
not go back to face the sentence.

The Fate of Chicken, Corn, and Pepper

Here is a burning tale!

By all means, tell us a burning tale!

Chicken, Corn, and Pepper were dear friends upon a time. They were so close friends that even water could not pass among them. They all lived in a big house. One day the Chicken was so ravenous (very hungry) she caught the Corn's child as well as the Pepper's child and ate them. This act led to a fight among the friends.

In anger Pepper poke a finger into the Chicken's eyes and broke them. Corn also picked a big heavy stick and hit the blinded Chicken, killing it in the act. In the evening their master returned home from the farm. He was very hungry as he had not eaten all day on the farm. When the master saw the dead Chicken, he asked who killed her.

Pepper informed their master that the Chicken ate their children.. Corn added that Pepper plucked out the Chicken eyes, and he Corn hit her with a stick. Their master became furious. He grinded Corn into a meal, crashed Pepper into a fine powder, and prepared the chicken. With the three ingredients he cooked a delicious food. He ate the food and watered it down with wine. After the meal, he was full and happy. He opined that the three friends would live happily together in his belly. The criminal as well as the victims who took the law into their own hands were punished.

Mankind's master is God. If we don't learn to live peacefully together, our ends will be as those three friends. The Creator will throw us into the Everlasting Hell Fire.

The Fate of Two Young Men

Here is a tale of Fate!

May we hear a tale of Fate!

A great many years ago, two young men lived in a far away city, their names were Mr. Mouse and Mr. Firefly. They were very poor and did odd jobs to make ends meet. Early one morning they set out to a distant town in search of a job they heard about. They traveled all day, in the evening, they decided to spend the night with strangers, then continue the journey the next day to the next town.

The two friends lodged with a man and his wife. The family welcomed the strangers warmly, and prepared a delicious meal for them. The meal consisted of corn bread, vegetables, and Kanami (aromatic, soft fried fish). A portion of the Kanami was eaten, the other portion was set aside for breakfast the next morning, before the young men leave. They all went to bed. However, in the middle of the night Mr. Mouse said something was smelling. He could not sleep as he realized the Kanami was stored in the same room they were. Eventually Mr. Mouse could no longer resist the temptation, he grabbed the fried fish and ate it.

The next morning their Hostess went to get the Kanami to fix breakfast, but no Kanami could be found. The Hostess was perplexed and inquired loud:

Where is Kanami?

Where is Kanami?

Mr. Firefly told her that Mr. Mouse ate it in the middle of the night. During the day, the young son of the family became very sick. In the evening Mr. Mouse told the family that Mr. Firefly was a Wizard, responsible for the child's sickness. When the Hostess stepped out into the darkness, there he was: The Wizard himself. Mr. Firefly was up and down intermittently lightning the darkness.

The Host called the two young men together. He said he was the individual in charge of Employment in the next town. In light of their stealing and wizardry, he would have nothing to do with them. They were asked to go back to where they came. They went home where they remained wretched to this day, due to stealing and wizardry.

How the Sheep
Became the Sacrificial Animal

Are you in the mood for a tale?

Yes, we are dying to hear a tale!

In the days of yore, in a far away Kingdom, there lived a King who ruled by edicts (orders). One of his orders was Death be caught and brought to him. Who ever did so would share half of his wealth. Three young men came forward, and said they would go to catch Death and bring it back to the King. The King accepted their offer. The King called a party with sumptuous food to celebrate their departure.

The three young men set out on a journey through the Kingdom. An elderly lady, they were unaware of, followed them. Four months they searched for Death but did not find Death. At the end of the fourth month, the older of the men got sick and died. The remaining two became afraid but continued on their quest. It wasn't long when the second young man too died. The third young man went on with the search alone. He was adamant, he had to find Death, he had to share in the wealth of the Kingdom. He traveled to several nearby Kingdoms.

One day at the fork in the road, he came upon the elderly lady that was shadowing them. The old lady asked the young man to go back home, in that, he would never catch Death. He became even more stubborn in the search. Eventually he arrived at a big river. He walked up and down the river bank looking for a way to cross it.

Along the bank he saw a bird, Ogoli, who handed the young man several sheep to take back to the King. And to let the King know that was what he found. The young man refused the offer. He insisted in crossing the river to the other side to catch Death. Half way in the river, he drowned.

There upon, the elderly lady took the sheep to the King. She informed the King that the three young men he sent to catch Death, did not make it back. The sheep were what they found, and she brought them to the King. She advised the King to raise the sheep to produce young ones. From hence forth, the sheep should be used in celebrations and as sacrificial animals.

Why We Have Bachelors
in the World

Let us spin a tale!
Go ahead!

In ancient times, there lived a man whose name was Uwozi. He was very rich and had everything he needed, yet could not find any woman to marry, due to his character. One day he went to his farm to dig potato. While digging he came across a small beautiful one, the like unknown.

Uwozi, *"Will this paragon of beauty become a woman for me to marry?"*
The Beautiful Potato, *"If I become a woman for you to marry, you will one day, when angry, insult me by calling me daughter of Potato."*

Uwozi, *"Never, I will not call you names, therefore be willing to become a woman for me to marry."*

The potato agreed and became a woman. Uwozi married her and took her home. At the moment of their arrival, all the town folks came to Uwozi's home to admire the gorgeous bride. Even after a whole month, people continued to come to gawk at the paragon of beauty.

Bird's eggs were the only food the wife ate. Hence everyday Uwozi was searching the woods for bird's eggs. Once while in the woods searching, he was beaten and soaked by rains. He returned home cold and hungry. His wife did not prepare hot water for his bath, let alone cook for him.

Uwozi was beside himself. He asked his wife, "how come you, a daughter of potato, look down on me?" He insulted his wife in a every which way. A moment later, the wife came out from the house and asked, "didn't I warn you not to call me a child of potato when angry? I am therefore going back to where I come from." The woman then ran away singing:

> *Potato, your husband insults you*
> *Potato, your husband insults you*
> *Beautiful Potato, your husband insults you*
> *Uwozi, bye-bye!*

The husband ran after her but could not catch up. Uwozi became a bachelor again, till the day he died. The fact that in anger, the Uwozis might insult their wives was the reason we have bachelors in the world.

The Origin of Crowing by Cocks

Here is a mythology!

May we hear a mythology!

In ancient times, in Western Europe, was a Kingdom called Angleterre. The Kingdom was ruled by Henry The Terrible. King Henry married six wives, one after the other. He was a ruthless ruler, mean to his subjects, and dangerous to his wives.

When ever he married, an order was secretly issued to the queen to have only daughters, and no sons. Henry feared sons would grow to rival him. The first wife had a daughter. A day was set and the daughter was brought before him at his court. The King was exceedingly happy. Mother and child were showered with expensive gifts.

However it was not long before the King found an attractive woman. He got rid of the queen and married this woman. The same secret order, same presentation at the court, same expensive gifts, and same fate happened to all the queens and their daughters, except the fourth queen. The forth queen had the misfortune of bearing a son. When mother and child were presented, the King became furious, he banished them from his Kingdom.

The citizens were astonished. They could not believe their ears. Yet none could say anything in the presence or behind Henry The Terrible. Finally Henry gave orders that his secret oath given to the queens be proclaimed to the nation. That the fourth queen violated the oath. Further more he ordered that no one should sympathize with nor help the banished mother and child.

The queen and the prince pitifully traveled through the country side, shunned and isolated. Eventually they came to a cave and made it their home. They were poor, destitute, and lived on wild fruits. Occasionally they received handouts from a few who dared to disobey the King's orders. The banished prince grew up in the cave, his expertise in hunting and gathering fruits sustained then.

One day the prince came face to face with a "Believe-it-or-not-countless-eyes."

There was no place on this scary thing without eyes. The prince was so afraid he turned round to rum away. The scary thing spoke, ordered him to stop, and to come nearer. In fear, the prince went nearer to the thing. The prince was handed a heavy gourd, an egg, and a magic wand. He was asked to go back to his mother and both should leave the cave. They should travel to wherever they wished, and when they got to a place the prince liked, he should smash the gourd and the egg on the ground.

The young prince went back to his mother and did exactly as he was commanded to do. The splitting gourd cleared the forest, and the shattering egg created a castle. The castle came complete with furnishing, guards, and servants. A small town evolved around the castle. The prince became King of the surrounding areas and his mother was in charge of the castle. They were blessed with riches and were exceedingly generous to their subjects.

Henry The Terrible heard of them. They were more powerful and richer than he was. Henry was angry and envious. He sent soldiers to destroy the prince and his Kingdom. The prince waved the magic wand in their faces. There upon the soldiers joined the prince and became his soldiers and subjects. He sent wave after wave of soldiers and courtiers but similar fate fell on all. The inevitable happened, Henry had no one left in his castle or Kingdom to obey him.

In the end Henry went to the prince. At the Gate, Henry shouted at the prince to give up. The prince over rode him with a commanding shout, picked the magic want, shook it, and hit the ground three times. Henry The Terrible became a very Big Cock. The prince ordered the Big Cock to be locked up in the chicken coop. The order was carried out immediately.

Early the next morning, the Big Cock crowed from the chicken coop, "Korkorliakoreh....!" The people woke up and went to their farms and places of work. From that day and even to this day, the cock wakes people up from their sleep with its crows.

Not long ago, my grandfather told me the story of a race of people called the English. The English went around the world conquering, subjecting, and insulting the people. It is high time the people poke fun at the English. Believe this myth at your own risk.

Why There Are No More Alligators in the Allegheny Mountains

Here is a remarkable tale!

Let's hear a tale!

A great many years ago, there was a Gullah fellow from Beaufort, South Carolina. His name was Ukawk and he loved to travel. He traveled through North Carolina, Virginia and Pennsylvania. He came back with fantastic stories. Here was one of the tales he loved to tell. The tale staggered out from the Cumberland Mountains of Tennessee, planted one foot on the Appalachian and Blue Ridge Mountains of North Carolina, and another foot on the Alleghenies of Virginia and Pennsylvania. In the Catskills of New York it came face to face with Rip Van Winkle playing a game of nine pins. It turned round, became unsteady, and fell prone (on its face) on the Alleghenies, on Alligators, and on Dutch Settlers of Pennsylvania.

In those days the Allegheny Mountains were populated by alligators (gators). The gators were everywhere, in the streams, rivers, lakes, and on top of the mountains. They roamed around freely, eating frogs, fishes, snakes, and small mammals. The Dutch settlers lived in towns and villages scattered in the valleys. They cultivated the land, planted tobacco, potatoes, corn and vegetables. The settlers did not bother the alligators and the alligators did not bother the settlers. The settlers called the mountains alligator mountains or simply alligators.

As time went on, a race of very destructive people called the English appeared. They were uncouth (lacking in polish and grace), uncultured, and roamed the high seas mostly as pirates. Some of them traded with the Dutch settlers as well as with the Native Americans for food and fur. Eventually a few of the English began to settle among the Dutch. Others followed the Native fur traders and trappers into the mountains. There they came face to face with the alligators; they had never seen gators before. However, they had been warned to stay away from the gators. The English, in their mispronunciation, called the alligators Alleghenies. In time, the name stuck, and everybody began calling the mountains Alleghenies.

The Dutch settlers wore wooden shoes. The English preferred leather shoes. There were no cattle in the Alleghenies to make hides out of as they did in their homeland. However, it did not take the English long to discover that hides could be made from alligator skins. The process was straight forward. The gator was killed, skinned, and the skin stretched out to dry. The dried skin became hide. At first shoes were made out of the hides, then handbags, then traveling boxes called portmanteau. Soon the English traders, sailors and buccaneers began a lucrative trade in gator hides.

The trade was so profitable that more English people came. They took the lands from the Dutch settlers and the Native Americans. As for the alligators they were destroyed, not a single one left. That was why there were no more alligators in the Alleghenies. This was a remarkable yarn spawned by the Gullah traveler from Beaufort, South Carolina.

Mud Island

Believe this tale at your own risk. Any where along the River Bank Drive and I-40 in down town, Memphis, Tennessee, one could see Mud Island. The Island was created by the Mighty Mississippi River eons ago. The Island was full of mud, nothing but mud, hence the name.

Not long ago, the city of Memphis was founded along the bank of the river. The city fathers met at City Hall to make laws. Whenever they were tired or shedding their duties, the aldermen would take boats and ferry themselves to Mud Island. There they would frolic and wrestle in the mud all day. As time went on, the aldermen could be seen frequently on the Island. They would rather be mud wrestling than make laws. Civic duties were neglected.

The people of Memphis, standing along the River Bank, could see what was going on in the mud but could do nothing. Imploring and chastising the law makers came to no avail. Then one day it happened. In a fit of anger, the people rose and built a bridge from down town Memphis to Mud Island. On the Island, they poured concrete, tons of concrete everywhere. They created River Tennessee with flowing water, right in the middle of the Mighty Mississippi.

The city aldermen could no longer go on retreat to Mud Island. It was said from that day, the aldermen applied themselves to their civic duties, enacting laws as honestly as politicians could be expected to do.

Crude Surgeons
on the Far Away Island of Aniloracs

Here is horrible tale!

We are not interested in a horrible tale!

You will hear it anyhow!

A great many years ago, on the far away Island of Anilo-racs, in the middle of Pacific Ocean, there lived two types of surgeons. The first group was composed of MD's. The MD's were medical doctors, licensed by the Island Government to perform surgeries. They used anesthesia, performed the incredible surgeries, and followed up with visits to the patients. The second group of surgeons comprised of alligators. The alligators were not licensed by the Island Government. However they performed surgeries on animals, fish, and even human beings. These unlicensed individuals, without the benefit of anesthesia, would crudely tear off a finger, an arm, a toe, or a leg of their victims. Their idea of followed up was to swallow the cut off limbs.

The Governor of the Island had warned this second group several times to stop performing the crude surgeries. But the alligators refused to listen. The alligators claimed they had been on the Island before human beings came. They proclaimed they were on the Island since the days of dinosaurs, and were not going to listen to nor obey human beings. One alligator was heard saying, it was human beings that were intruding on their territories.

The Governor was taken aback at the brazenness of the gators. He too issued proclamation. He proclaimed that any one found guilty performing crude surgery should be put to death. The crime had to be committed before the punishment. People were therefore, warned, not to become victims.

The alligator was an efficient killing machine. On each side was a pair of legs. Each leg had five claws capable of tearing any animal apart. The rear end was a deadly tail used in swimming and administering blows on the head of victims. In front of the alligator well, you don't want to find out, and you don't want to be there.

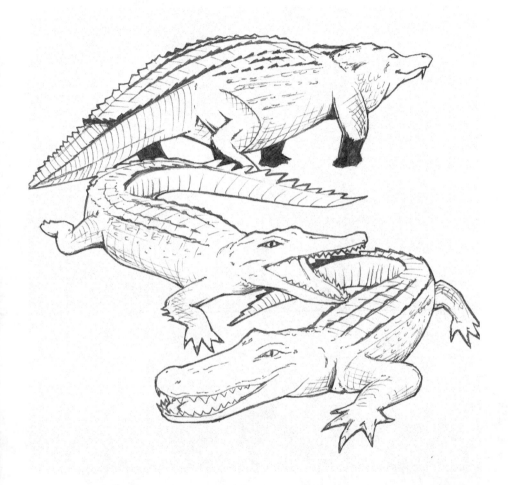

UFO Over Scott Community on St. Helena Island

The St. Helena Island and The Lady's Island, off the coast of South Carolina, are flyway zones. On any given day, one can see jet liners flying thirty five to forty five thousand feet above, heading North from Florida and Latin America. The clouds they part trail behind them. The trails begin as straight lines then zigzag as the winds blow them. It is a beautiful sight in the morning when several streaks are crafted in the sky.

Several feet below the jet liners are another group of air crafts. These are small engine planes carrying two to four passengers. They do not leave trails, they fly below the clouds. They can clearly be seen and the noises they make are deadening. Some of these planes land on Lady's Island Airport while others land on Hilton Head Island Airport.

On first June 1993 the weather was clear, no clouds or rains, only the warm sun that morning. Several kids from Lady's Island and St. Helena Island were playing base ball game at Scott Community Sports Complex, on St. Helena Island. The parents that brought the kids were on the side lines, cheering them up.

The spectators heard faint distant sound that came closer and closer. Within minutes every one at the Sport Complex could hear the loud, metallic sound of a giant aircraft. The saucer like craft appeared barely above the trees, in a second, it flew over the Complex and disappeared . The people at the game that fateful morning heard a deadening crash in the nearby tomato farm.

The kids, their parents, and the nearby residents rushed to the field. But they did not see anything. Some one had called 911. The rescue personnel: fire trucks, ambulance and the Sheriff Deputies came immediately to the farm. The people mingled among the uniformed personnel searching around the farm. However no craft was seen. The surrounding woods and farms were also searched but no air craft was seen. After a while, the people began to wonder. The rescue personnel thought the call was a hoax. Suddenly, the tomato bushes began to bend and shake.

Right in the middle of the farm, in full view of all present, a giant camouflaged saucer-like UFO rose, with deadening sound, flew high above the trees, and disappeared over the horizon.

Why No More Dogs
on Ashley McKee Plantation

Are you ready for a tale?

We are dying to hear a tale!

This was a tale, that was real, that was told, and that was forgotten. On the Ashley McKee Plantation of Lady's Island, people lived in cottages on their own lands. The cottages were surrounded by woods and far from one another. The people raised chickens in their back yards, and worked in the city of Beaufort as carpenters, bricklayers, domestics, school teachers, and veterinarians. From morning till evening the cottages were empty as the people had gone away to work. For safety and security of themselves at night as well as their properties in the day time, the people hired trusted security guards.

The guards patrolled the cottages and visited one another nearby. Sometimes they could be seen in groups but they did their work eagerly and honestly. In the evening and on Saturdays the children played games with the security guards. The games were held on front porches and on front yards. The most popular games were running and racing. The guards always won. They could be heard laughing, barking, and jumping around after each game. It was not the fault of the guards that the kids had two legs, running against the four legged guards. You see, the guards were family dogs.

Then it began to happen. The dogs were disappearing. The people looked for their pets everywhere but no trace of them. They checked with the veterinaries in the area as well as the animal shelter near the Air Station but to no avail.

Housing development came to Lady's Island in leaps and bounds. Construction workers were all over the Island. In clearing the land and digging foundations for new homes, workers discovered several bones. More bones were found along the creeks and in the marshes. The bones were easily identified as dog bones. But how and why dog bones, the people then remembered their lost dogs.

The clearing of lands deprived alligators of their habitat. They began roaming around trying to find answers to their dilemma. One day a contractor's truck ran over an alligator. In its belly were dog bones. The news spread like forest fire. The fate of the dogs was finally solved. The alligators ate the dogs. To this day, there are no more dogs in the Ashley McKee Plantation.

What Children Say

We took our son John to church a lot. We went with him as a baby, toddler, three and four years old. At the age of four, he could sing several of the children's songs as well as imitate the ministers in preaching. He loved to preach. Hence we bought him a toy microphone. He would stand on a milk carton, or a chair, or on the bed and preach.

James, a family friend, began calling John a preacher. One day, James came by the house. After the usual greetings, he turned to John and said, "hey preacher, how do you do?" John said, "fine." When James left, John came closer to me and said, "he called me a preacher, but I am a pastor." What four years old know and can say is astonishing.

The Listening Power of a Child

We just moved into a new home in the country with three months old baby. As new parents we took everything seriously to make the home livable. To smooth the yard, bushes were cleared and soil moved around. Stubs, roots, and dead trees were removed. We bought new furniture, appliances and pictures. Four years later, the baby became a child following me around the yard.

In our back yard was a little garden with tomatoes, okra, bell pepper and corn. A lot of time was spent in the garden. Several giant water-oaks were in the yard; one in particular had dead branches and live branches. Afraid that the dead branches would fall on some one, we decided to kill the tree. About six inches band of barks were removed around the tree. A few weeks later, all the leaves turned brown.

I was in the garden one afternoon when John, now four years old, pulled beside me. He pointed at the dead leaves at the top of the tree and asked, "Daddy, what happened to the tree?" I answered, "I killed the tree." John then said, "Daddy, the Church says don't kill." I was dumbfounded, four years old teaching me a lesson from the church! John went to church every Sunday, but little did we know he was listening to the sermons.

Human Being Is Not Trustworthy

Here are some sayings!

We want to hear some aphorisms!

People, fear Human Being

His mouth is sweet

His heart is clouded.

His word is one thing

His thought is another.

People, fear Human Being.

People, fear Human Being

When you have good thoughts towards Him

He answers with bad thoughts.

When you do Him a favor

He claps the back of His hands.

People, fear Human Being

People, fear Human Being

When you are in fortunes, He knows you

When you are in misfortunes, He turns His back.

He is many sided Being

One cannot enumerate them.

People, fear Human Being

The Dual World

Here are some clichés!
We prefer adages!
You will hear both!

My friends, remember we live in a Dual World

There is the sky and there is the earth

There is dusk and there is dawn

There is a time to sleep and a time to rise

There is raining season and there is dry season

There is sowing season and there is reaping season

There is a time of famine and a time of plenty

There is a time of merriment and a time of anger.

My friends, remember we live in a Dual World

There are small things and there are large things

There are grown ups and there are children

There are elephants and there are mice

There are worms and there are mites

There are platters and there are Monkish Dishes

There are mortars and there are pestles

There are bracelets and there are rings

My friends, remember we live in a Dual World

If today is not good

Tomorrow will be better

Today it is a dream

Tomorrow it will be reality

Forward is the march

Hard work leads to success

We live in a Dual World.

Epilogue

BOGO PEOPLE

Bogo people are located in the western Plateau section of Togo, in the region of West Africa, and on the Continent of Africa. One is not to confuse the small nationality of Bogo with the country of Togo. They love mountains and live in the Ghana Togo Mountain Ranges.

By race and ethnicity, they are West African people and speak a West African language. The nationality is Bogo, the people are Bogo (plural), and the language is IGO. The language is one of the unique languages where all nouns begin with vowels and most end in vowels. All verbs begin with consonants. Any deviation from above means the noun or verb is a foreign one. IGO is a living language and borrows words from nearby languages, from English and French, and from Hebrew for religious services.

Bogo people are indigenous to the area, not recent arrivals. There are about 5 to 6 thousands of them, living mostly in Togo. However, some can be found in Ghana, Benin, Europe, and in America.

Bogo people are religious; there are no known atheists among them. About 15 percent practice the traditional religion. About 85 percent are Christians, mostly Protestants, then Evangelicals, and Roman Catholics.

They are agrarian farmers (own their lands), who grown cash crops of coffee and cocoa; and food crops, mostly mountain rice, cassava and vegetables. The alternative to the harsh mountain farming is education. Bogo people love education and have attained all levels of education. Among them are doctors, college professors, ambassadors, lawyers, a few politicians, teachers, etc.

Bogo people have their own culture and customs. They love music, singing, and dancing. They also love to express their world view through telling Folk Tales.

Illustrations

Illustrations on pages 35, 36 and 42 are by
Brenda Singleton.

The remainder of illustrations are by John
Drawingman Bradley.

Brenda is an art teacher in Beaufort County School System.
John is a resident artist in Beaufort. Both are Gullahs, living on Gullah Shining Shores.

Printed in the USA
CPSIA information can be obtained
at www.ICGtesting.com
LVHW011236230823
756032LV00004B/163